THE APES OF DEVIL'S ISLAND

The Darkness at Windon Manor

BY MAX BRAND

The Exploits of Beau Quicksilver

BY FLORENCE M. PETTEE

The Flying Legion

BY GEORGE ALLAN ENGLAND

The Golden Cat:
The Adventures of Peter the Brazen, Volume 3

BY LORING BRENT

The Opposing Venus: The Complete Cabalistic Cases
of Semi Dual, the Occult Detector

BY J.U. GIESY AND JUNIUS B. SMITH

The Radio Menace

BY RALPH MILNE FARLEY

The Ruby of Suratan Singh: The Adventures
of Scarlet and Bradshaw, Volume 2

BY THEODORE ROSCOE

The Sheriff of Tonto Town:
The Complete Tales of Sheriff Henry, Volume 2

BY W.C. TUTTLE

The Vengeance of the Wah Fu Tong:
The Complete Cases of Jigger Masters, Volume 1

BY ANTHONY M. RUD

THE APES OF DEVIL'S ISLAND

JOHN CUNNINGHAM

ALTUS PRESS
2018

PUBLISHING HISTORY

"The Apes of Devil's Island" originally appeared in the April 7, 14, 21, and 28, 1923 issues of *Argosy* magazine (Vol. 150, No. 4–Vol. 151, No. 1). Copyright © 1923 by The Frank A. Munsey Company. Copyright renewed © 1950 and assigned to Steeger Properties, LLC. All rights reserved.

THANKS TO

Joel Frieman & Janice Roberts

Visit *altuspress.com* for more books like this.

CHAPTER I

A MYSTERY

THE WIND THAT had tumbled down the cloud-burdened mountains and had rushed across the white-capped lake was howling and moaning under the eaves of my cottage. Two days ago the first frost had arrived, and the forests were now splotched with red and yellow. Before long that gay assemblage which had formed the summer colony at Saranac Inn would be dissipated to the four corners of the globe. It made me lonely to think of parting with all my friends of the summer: some I might run across in the city, others never see again.

As I looked out upon the wind-lashed September lake, I marveled at the contrast it offered to the quiet, balmy August lake. It was no more than three weeks ago that Eleanor Meredith and I had sat in a canoe, watching the moonlight play over the calm surface dotted with lily pads, with the dark shadows of the woods behind.

As she leaned back against the cushions, her white satiny dress had fallen gracefully about her slender body, offsetting the jet of her dark hair. It was not going to be easy to say good-by to Eleanor. Besides her good looks, she was a good sport and possessed an understanding nature. Her father and mother also were very pleasant, and I would miss seeing them. There were many others at the inn whom I had learned to like and with whom I would soon have to part. I looked out of the window, and sadly viewed the harbingers of winter. The telephone bell rang shrilly. Taking off the receiver, I heard Eleanor's cheery voice.

"'Lo, Jimmy Wendell?" she called. "Father's decided to go cruising in Florida for a couple of months, and wants to know whether you'd like to go, too."

"Sure thing," I answered. "Well, that is—I mean who is going? And when?"

"We're all going," she said. "Mother, Dad, Nicky and I. We'll probably leave for Miami in about three weeks."

"Great!" I answered. "Of course I'd be just crazy to go. Sure I'm not imposing? Say, who's Nicky, or Micky, or whatever you called him?"

"He's my brother; his real name is George. Dad says to come to the cottage and we'll talk the cruise over."

"All right," I answered. "Be right over."

The raindrops were still tapping at the window pane and the wind roared as raucously as ever, but somehow it now produced an effect of open hearth, chestnut-and-cider autumn, rather than of loneliness. It is strange what one little telephone bell can accomplish.

As I slipped into my raincoat and drew on my galoshes I marveled at the abrupt manner in which a tropical cruise had loomed upon my horizon. A matter which was equally astonishing was the fact that Eleanor had a brother. Queer I'd never heard him mentioned before, I thought.

And now you know why autumn found me at Eagle Crest, the Meredith's home on Long Island. I was spending a week with them, and then we were all to board the train that would take us to Miami.

I believe that it is customary in books for the "I" character to give his pedigree, a more or less brief account of his infancy, childhood, boyhood, and all the other "hoods." However, in my case it will be sufficient to say that I am very much like the rest of you, and have probably done, said and felt the same things

you have. I was twenty at the time I am speaking of, and had just graduated from college. So much for "me."

Now, nothing is better for the appetite than a brisk walk before breakfast. About the third day of my visit I came to the realization of this fact, and went for an early morning stroll in the large gardens. The dew sparkled on the grass, and the whole world smelled and looked its sweetest. Such surroundings are conducive to dreaming, and I fell victim to the spell. As I ambled along, plucking an unoffending shoot here and there, I painted bright pictures of the future.

However, I was soon deflected from this train of musing by the sight of a small figure bending over a table some distance ahead. I supposed it was Nicky. Although I had not seen him yet, I knew that he was at Eagle Crest. It struck me as a strange thing that he did not eat with the rest of the family; he certainly was old enough; twelve is a very advanced age for the nursery.

At all events, this was a good chance to make Nicky's acquaintance, so I walked across the grass toward him. As I drew near it was evident that the boy was not aware of my presence; he could not hear my footfalls on the lawn, and was very much engrossed with something before him. Having a natural interest in children, I stepped up to within a couple of paces of him, and peered over his shoulder. To say that I was surprised would be putting it mildly.

I was almost shocked at Nicky's occupation. There, pinned to the table, was a large horsefly. The little devil was engaged in a systematic devastation of its legs and wings; after each removal he would bend eagerly forward for a closer view of the struggles of the hapless fly. I admit I was fascinated by the proceedings, and determined to keep quiet and see them through. When no more limbs remained to be removed, the young scalawag proceeded with apparent gusto to twist the head from the mutilated body.

And then, while the miserable insect was still twitching, he snatched it up and carried it swiftly toward his mouth. He was going to eat it!

This was too much for me. Stepping forward, I knocked the fly from his clutch with a quick slap. The effect on him was as astonishing as it was unexpected. With a snarl the little body sprang aside and settled into a low crouch. His small face, with its beady eyes, was contorted by a malevolent frown. He made it very apparent how much my interference was resented, and awed me terribly by the savagery of his expression.

Then his aspect suddenly changed, and I beheld in front of me only a frightened boy. He appeared very natural and child-like as he hesitated a moment, and then said simply:

"Please don't tell them. If you do, I Shall be punished."

I assured the youngster that I would say nothing about the matter if he would refrain from such actions in the future. With that he turned and ran toward the house. As he hastened away I followed him with my eyes.

He was about the average size for a child of twelve, but I noticed that his arms were abnormally long, and dangled at his sides in a peculiar manner as he ran. When he disappeared from sight I returned to my walk, and marveled at the strange things children will do.

THE MEREDITH house—castle would come closer to describing it—was situated on a quasi cliff overlooking the Sound. The grading of the lawn had necessitated a concrete retaining wall which on the inner side was about three feet high; on the outer side it dropped sheer down for thirty feet, and was then hidden from sight by a dense tangle of trees and bushes. It became an after-dinner custom with me to sit on this wall with my coffee cup in hand, and chat with Nicky.

The little chap had quite captivated my heart, and it was impossible to reconcile myself to the fact that this affable little boy was the same being that I had seen one morning not long before. Through constant association with Nicky, that first picture I had of him was slowly fading from my memory. All the Merediths were in better spirits than I had ever seen them before, and could not get enough of Nicky's company. I believe they were fonder of their son than any family I have ever seen. They treated him like a child that had just recovered from a hopeless illness. This idea struck me so forcibly that I asked Eleanor if Nicky had not been quite ill lately.

My question was met with a startled glance and an ejaculation. "Why? What makes you think so?"

It was so evident that Eleanor meant an emphatic negation that I thought it wise to let the matter drop by merely saying:

"He doesn't look very strong. I thought it more than likely that he had not been well."

In my talks with Nicky I found that he was very bright and interesting. His puckered little face and his dangling arms gave him a kind of fascination that kept him from becoming tedious like most boys of his age. I had not seen any more indications of a love of inflicting pain, and was beginning to think that Nicky had taken my advice to heart. However, my hopes were doomed to a disillusioning blow. It came about this way.

Having been so delighted with my pre-breakfast walks, I suggested to Eleanor that she accompany me. She fell in with my proposal, and for a couple of mornings we had walked about, getting our feet wet in the dew.

One morning as we ambled along, laughing and chattering about nothing in particular, I espied Nicky in the distance. The sight of him leaning over a table filled me with vague misgivings. I did my utmost to turn Eleanor in another direction, but I was unable; she insisted on going straight ahead.

Finally the inevitable happened, and she saw Nicky.

"Looks interested, doesn't he?" she said with a mischievous smile; then added: "Let's sneak up and see what he is doing."

All I could say to dissuade her was of no avail. I contemplated coughing loudly, or making some commotion to attract Nicky's attention, for I felt instinctively that he was about something forbidden. However, I remembered that Eleanor knew more about Nicky than I did; and besides, she was his sister, so I let her have her way, and we walked guardedly toward the stooping form.

This would be a splendid time for a great deal of morbid detail. But I think it will be enough to say that Nicky was literally tearing a live squirrel to pieces. The poor animal was tied down, and its mouth stuffed with a handkerchief to muffle its agonizing wails; its struggles were pitiful to see.

Eleanor burst into tears at the sight, and seized Nicky roughly. He was again as I had first seen him. His ugly, snarling face was covered with blood; he was fighting his sister and doing his best to tear himself free from her hold. Eleanor, however, was stronger than he, and it was apparent that his attempts would be useless. She turned her white face to me, and, pointing to the mangled squirrel, whispered:

"Put that out of its misery—and I'll take this to the house."

I BREAKFASTED by myself that day. When morning was fading into afternoon the butler informed me that the family were lunching in their rooms, and that I could have lunch wherever I wished. I chose the most unexpected place—the dining room.

The first company I had was at dinner. Dr. and Mrs. Meredith and Eleanor were at the table. They pretended to eat, but at best it was but a sorry meal. Dr. and Mrs. Meredith exchanged meaning glances, and Eleanor tried to make conversation with me. I was glad when the repast was over, and we went out on to the lawn in the cool of the evening for coffee. Eleanor and I sat apart on the wall, and for a long while were silent. She was the first to speak.

"It's such a shame. He seemed to be getting along so well."

No doubt my face showed my intense curiosity to know what it was all about, for Eleanor put her hands on mine and said:

"I'd like to explain things to you. They are so odd. Father says he is sure it is so, yet he doubts his own belief, and so far has told no one but the family."

With that she sighed; then, turning abruptly on her heel, she walked slowly away toward the house, leaving me in the gathering gloom.

CHAPTER II

A BLOW IN THE DARK

OUR TRIP SOUTH was uneventful; the same old dirt, cinders, cards, and telegraph poles. However, there was one happening that should not be put in the category of the uneventful. This was Dr. Meredith's discovery that an old medical school friend was on the train—a Dr. Grame. He was a big, intelligent, uncouth man, with baggy trousers and abrupt manners; but there was a charm and interest about him that attracted instantly.

In spite of his noisy blustering, he was, according to Dr. Meredith, one of the country's greatest men in his line; but Dr. Meredith neglected to say what his line was. The two doctors spent a great deal of their time together, and when we were nearing our destination Dr. Meredith told us with satisfaction that he had persuaded his friend to accompany us on the cruise.

At Miami we put in a day shopping and looking around. The yacht was in commission. This was a great surprise. In Florida, if a boat is in running shape within two weeks of the promised time, the owner is rightfully entitled to boast himself a favorite of the gods. Rejoicing in such unusual dry-dock punctuality as a good omen, we turned our bow toward the southeast early the next morning.

A smart breeze whipped up the surface of the water into gay, dancing waves that sparkled beneath the bright sun and cloudless sky. The distant keys showed up fresh green, with an occasional white house snuggling close down to the water. On such a morning it was impossible not to be happy.

We tried to start a game of bridge on the after-deck, but the increasing strength of the wind rendered it very difficult to keep the cards on the table. Playing under such annoying conditions is no pleasure, so we gave the game up.

Dr. Meredith and Dr. Grame retired to a couple of deck chairs, and began one of those long discussions in medical terms which are intelligible only to the initiated. Mrs. Meredith evidently experienced a kind of call of the wild, and turned her energies to knitting socks for no one in particular. Nicky, who had been rather subdued lately, collected the scattered pack and made straight for the cabin, to dream over the architectural difficulties of constructing an extensive mansion of cards.

Eleanor and I wandered aimlessly forward, getting a pair of binoculars as we passed the cabin. Picking up the channel stakes was great fun for nearly an hour, until we plowed into the Gulf Stream. Then there were no more stakes to pick up and it was getting so rough that leaning over the rail to sweep the horizon with the glasses was extremely foolhardy.

We made our way back to the leeward side of the cabin, and stretched out in steamer chairs. We talked and gabbled away about everything and nothing as young people will, and passed the time enjoyably enough. The rolling of the boat was increasing perceptibly, and the wind contained a more strident note as it tore around the corner of the cabin.

When a grinning Japanese steward, in spotless white, came to announce that luncheon was awaiting us, I realized I was ravenous—and boasted of my desire to eat an elephant. But alas, the scriptures are only too literal when they state that pride goeth before a fall. Mine came with a vengeance. No sooner had I attacked my third piece of roast beef than I suddenly and acutely noticed the abominable rolling of the boat. Through the port-hole I could see the horizon mount swiftly toward the zenith, and then subside sickeningly. I stood it for several moments, and then was forced to take French leave.

The rough weather continued for four days while I endured agony. The fifth day was comparatively calm, and I convalesced on deck while we lay at anchor in the lee of a sheltering island. The Meredith family, with the exception of Nicky, were still confined to their beds.

In spite of myself I could not but feel gratified at this; for since I was the first to take to my bed, it was fitting that I should be the first back on deck. It had always been a theory with me that to succumb to seasickness was the rankest unmanliness. Although I now realized that I had formed my ideas without any basis of experience, still it was comforting to know that I had not been sick any longer than the rest. As for Nicky, he did not count. I believe his stomach was as leathery as his face.

Just before sunset one of the yacht's launches appeared around a promontory of the island, and bobbed along toward us. As I stood and watched the boat, wondering where it had been and who was aboard it, the captain strolled up.

He was a big fellow with a strong square face, and hair tinged with gray above the temples; a man of some education and seemingly an efficient captain. Dr. Meredith had told me that he had had the captain for ten years or more, and held him to be indispensable. The only other thing I knew of him was that he was a great pal of Nicky's. When the captain was not busy he spent a great deal of his time with the youngster constructing miniature ships and spinning strange yarns.

"They've been harpooning. Looks as though they've got something."

"What did they go after?" I asked.

"Sawfish, porpoises, whip rays—anything big enough to attract a man eater."

"Man eater?" I queried.

"Yes, man-eating sharks. We cut up whatever we grain, and the tide carries out the blood and oil. The sharks scent it, and it attracts them to the boat. Then we will show you some sport. How would you like to have a nice pair of shark jaws that you could pass right over your body without touching your sides?"

"Are their jaws really that large?"

I thought he was telling the truth, but you can never tell about those who have a touch of salt in their makeup.

"Certainly," he replied earnestly. "They even come very much larger than that. If you cut out the jaws of a sixteen foot Leopard Shark, and open them, you will find that they will form a circle with a diameter of two feet or more; large enough to swallow a man whole, should the beast be inclined. However, they usually prefer to snap off a leg or two by way of getting up an appetite for their meal."

"Playful little things," I thought; then aloud, "And do you propose to rid the world of a few of these leopards to-night?"

"Yes, unless Dr. Meredith wants to move on to a quieter anchorage. I believe we are going to have more wind."

At this I groaned.

"Even if we do move off," went on the captain, "we can tow the porpoises, and the sharks will probably follow us."

By this time the launch was within hailing distance.

"Get anything?" bellowed the captain.

One of the men in the boat held up three fingers and shouted, "Two saws and a porpoise."

The captain turned to me and explained that when you get one "saw "you usually get its mate, especially at this time of the year.

"Does that apply to sharks also?" I asked.

"I really don't know," he answered, "but I don't believe so."

The captain and I moved to the stern in response to a call from the harpooners, and made their painter fast to a cleat.

"Shall we rip 'em, sir?" asked one of the sailors.

"Sure," answered his officer, "and do it well, George."

As George pulled the huge fish alongside the launch and

began to work on them, I noticed he had a very likable face, deeply furrowed by the lines that a smile naturally brings to the features.

In a few minutes the "ripping "was accomplished, and the two sailors came on deck wiping their hands on their trousers.

"I'd hate to be swimming around here in a couple of hours," remarked George as he went into the engine room to wash up.

The Merediths had not entirely recovered by dinner time, so the captain hauled anchor and set off for calmer waters. After a hearty meal, I went on deck to watch the scenery, and smoke. The wind had freshened a bit and was raising small waves on the surface of the water. The moon was shining brightly; small white clouds crossed its face now and then, casting dark shadows on the water.

Beyond the island, the wind was lashing the sea into white fury. I was very thankful that we were in a lee, as I watched the angry white-capped waves streaming out as though pursuing some unseen prey. As they came around the end of the island, they resembled a boiling mountain torrent as it lashes its way between the rocks and over falls. However, the water about us became quieter as we advanced. Leaning over the railing, I could plainly see the sawfish and porpoise we had harpooned in the afternoon, as they trailed through the water behind us at the end of a rope.

As I watched, there appeared a black shadow in the water and a darkish bulk came to the surface in a rush and flurry of water. There was a tremendous swirling on the surface and then a resounding snap. The form disappeared, taking half of the porpoise with it. Other dark forms were visible near the boat; they faded and grew strong again as the sharks took to deep water or approached the surface. I wondered how many there were, and tried to count the shadows. However, they shifted and faded so surreptitiously that I could come to no satisfactory conclusion.

Another one of the great beasts found the dead fish; there

was another rush, swirl and snap. I shuddered as I saw the back ripped from one of the sawfish. Thinking how helpless one would be in the water with these tigers of the deep, I was seized with a great repugnance for my proximity to the rail. So I turned and sought a steamer chair nearer the center of the boat.

There were two figures moving about up forward; one a sailor, coiling ropes near the bow. The other looked to me like Nicky, but I could not be certain, as a black cloud had momentarily obscured the moon. He was wandering around with his hands in his pockets, evidently doing nothing.

I thought of the sharks again, and could not resist the impulse to take another look at them. So I made my way aft, and peered down into the water. However, no shadows were visible. Thus disappointed, I wandered back to the cabin and decided I would crawl up the stairs to the chart house to have a chat with the captain.

I did not feel like turning in and had to admit to myself that I felt my nerves—doubtless because of the sharks. Besides, I imagined that I would find the captain's company quite interesting. However, the chart house was empty, except for the sailor at the wheel, who told me that the captain was below. I crawled back to the deck and went aft.

As I watched our wake streaming out behind us, frothing in the moonlight like fairy bubbles, I thought of Dr. Grame. I had seen very little of him—he seemed to be continually occupied with his host. What was it these two were so absorbed in which would bear discussion day after day? Could it be Nicky?

It was highly improbable that the ephemeral cruelty of a little boy could give two men of science such concern. Everyone knows that the majority of little boys go through a period when their chief delight is torturing insects. Some have this passive instinct more acutely than others; Nicky seemed to be among those in whom it had taken deepest root. However, it was nothing to worry about, and so I decided that it must be the discussions of various interesting problems of their profession which kept them so engrossed in conversation.

Dr. Grame was certainly a peculiar man. Although he was highly cultured, he had the most remarkable lack of manners I have ever seen in any one who was theoretically a gentleman. At times I was inclined to believe that this was a pose—his rudeness was studied; merely a means of attracting attention.

When he argued, he would thump his great fists on the arm of his chair till it rattled; at the table it was his custom to blow his nose with a great blast—and he would loudly make the most paradoxical statements, and then peer around eagerly, obviously hoping that some one would dispute him. Yet he had a tremendous amount of common sense, and was undeniably a great authority on some branch of science. It occurred to me that I must try to see more of this man, and find out what his "line" was; at least he was interesting and might prove—

"Help—damnation!"

I was roused from my musing by this shout from up forward. As I rushed up, it was followed by other more urgent and profane cries for aid. I reached the bow and called out. An answering shout came from over the side of the boat. Looking over the rail, I saw a man clinging to the guy wire that ran from the short bowsprit to a bolt in the hull. Part of his body was in the water, and he seemed to be having hard work to keep his hold.

"My left arm is hurt," he gasped, "help me up."

I could not reach him from the deck, so I hastily crawled out on to one of the upper stays, which ran from the bowsprit to the cut-water. I could not reach the man yet, and was beginning to crawl to the lower stay when he shouted and pointed to the right. I looked and experienced a dizzy sensation as I saw a large triangular fin cutting the water; it was coming toward us, and swiftly.

If the shark continued in the same direction, I knew I would not have time to reach the lower stay and pull the sailor up. So

I did the next best thing. Catching the wire rope firmly with both hands, I lowered myself till my feet were in the water. Then I swung myself forward and locked my legs around the man's body, just under his arms. He realized what I was doing, and grasped me around the waist. With a tremendous effort, I pulled myself up till my chin was level with the stay, and slipped my left arm over it.

Knowing that I could hold on in this position a minute or so, I looked down and saw that the sailor had drawn his legs up clear of the water. As I looked, the fin appeared again, directly underneath us, darting about swiftly. It was far from a pleasant sight. By this time the steersman had arrived. He had left his post on seeing what was happening, as we were in deep water and there were no reefs very near. He gave me a hand with the other sailor, and we were soon back on deck again.

The man who had fallen overboard—it was George—rubbed his arm and muttered:

"That was some close shave!"

"Is your arm hurt much, do you think?" I inquired.

"No," he replied, "just hit it on the stay and put it out of business for a while. Lucky for me it *did* hit the stay."

"How did you happen to fall overboard?"

"Fall overboard?" he replied, his face wrinkling into a puzzling grin. "I didn't fall overboard."

"Well, how did you get on the stays, then? I don't suppose you climbed there?"

The man hesitated, as if unwilling to disclose what was in his mind. Finally he beckoned to me, and walked off. As I followed him out of the hearing of the other sailor, George called out to his comrade, "Did you see me go over?"

The man replied that he had seen nothing. This, apparently, made George still more reluctant. He rubbed his chin reflectively, and said:

"Now look, sir, it ain't wise for me to say what I think. There ain't no evidence, so there you are. But I'll just tell you this—I didn't *fall* overboard. But if you want to do me a favor, you can just let the captain and the folks *think* I fell overboard."

He made a motion as if to leave, but lingered. Hesitating, he said: "Please, sir, be very careful not to mention this business about being pushed to the captain, will you?"

His tone was so beseeching that I was struck by it.

"Why don't you want him to know?" I could not refrain from inquiring.

"Well," he said, falteringly, "you know—now look, if he heard I said that, he'd think I was dotty, or had been drinking, and I'd get in trouble. You'll save me my job by not mentioning this pushing business." He fingered his arm gingerly, and said:

"Now, I guess I'll go below and get a drink—I need one."

I knew he was holding back something, and I did my best to get the man to tell me what was on his mind; but he absolutely refused to talk any more about the matter. As he left me, he called back:

"I've given ye a hint, and that's all I'll say. But as a friend, I say to ye, if you're goin' to stay on deck, *look out*."

And with that he stalked away.

I was absolutely nonplused. However, one thing was certain; George evidently thought that he had been pushed overboard by some one. I had seen no one on deck except Nicky; and surely he could not have been the author of such an attempt. However, I remembered the two times I had seen the child in the garden on Long Island. The more I thought the whole matter over, the more convinced I became that Nicky was the logical suspect.

The matter was grave, and demanded immediate action. Although I would have liked to shirk, I knew that it was up to me to investigate. So I took off my shoes, and crept down the stairs to my room, where I attached an old hunting knife to my belt. I felt that it was best to be armed in such affairs; for there was no telling who might be involved in the attempted murder, or to what lengths they might not go.

Nicky slept alone in a room directly off the lower cabin, and connecting with the room of his parents. As I approached the door, I tried to invent some excuse for entering his room at such a time, in case I should awaken his father or mother. Peculiarly enough, a feeling of guilt stole over me as I reached out my hand.

The knob worked easily, and I was inside without the slightest noise. Standing still until my eyes should become entirely accustomed to the dark, I could hear his regular breathing. I listened intently for similar noises from the adjoining room, but heard nothing. When I could distinctly make out his bed, I tiptoed to it, and saw him lying on his side, evidently sound asleep.

I was perfectly aware that there was a way of discovering whether he had really been in bed long enough to go to sleep, or whether he had just crawled under the covers and was pretending sleep; if I should place my hand under his body, warm bedclothes would be the proof that he had been in bed some time—cold ones would convict him. If he should awaken—well I would tell him something or other that would satisfy his curiosity; sleepy children are not hard to convince. If he were awake anyway, that would be a different story. So I slipped my hand very easily under him; the sheet was warm.

Nicky was not the one who had pushed George over. I was tremendously relieved, and quietly slipped out of his room. The question now was: what was to be done next? The only other person I could possibly suspect, other than some member of the crew, was Dr. Grame. But with all his outward brusqueness and bad manners, he certainly could not be capable of a deed like this. And where was any motive?

There was nothing to do but think matters over; perhaps George had not been pushed at all. He was probably chagrined at such carelessness, and wished to be mysterious in order to create a little excitement. So I went quietly on deck to reflect a little before I did anything foolish. As I walked up and down, I kept George's warning in mind, and had a sharp eye open.

I was satisfied that Nicky was innocent. Then the guilty man, if indeed there was any guilty man, must have been one of the crew. In that case, George would be the best source of information. One of the sailors probably had some grudge against him—if so, he, and he only, was in danger. This was a selfish thought, but it was comforting when I considered Eleanor and her parents.

I felt a desire to smoke and I drew out my pipe. As I filled it, I thought what a horrible fate George had narrowly escaped. My old curiosity about the sharks was roused again, so I went aft to see if they were still trailing the mangled sawfish. However, before I got near the railing, I took a good look to make sure no one was crouching in the shadow. I leaned against the railing, but could see nothing of the sharks. My pipe had gone out, so I bent over to strike a match.

As I did so, there was a loud crash behind me. I jumped nervously, and dropped the match. A sort of granular shiver ran through my chest. Wrenching myself around with fists clenched, ready for a fight, I saw quickly what had made the noise, and relaxed into a weak laugh. The wind had blown over one of the steamer chairs with a considerable crash. I replaced the chair, and derided myself for being a nervous cat.

In passing the cabin, I was seized with a fit of laughter; but it was the strangest I had ever experienced. As I opened my mouth, the earth seemed to shake, my head expanded to several times its normal size, and my knees sagged. I told myself that I had been hit on the head. And then there was a blank.

When my consciousness returned I was falling rapidly, and thought I heard some one weeping. The next moment I experienced a terrific shock, and found myself beneath the cold water, struggling frantically to rise.

CHAPTER III

A FIGHT FOR LIFE

ON COMING TO the surface, my first thought was to cry for help; and so I did, to the full extent of my water-soaked lungs. But it was all to no avail—the black letters on the stern of the Mermaid grew smaller and smaller; I was shouting against the wind, and there was no one on deck. I was left behind.

The dark outline of an island on the right cheered me up somewhat. It looked about a quarter of a mile away. I struck out strongly in that direction. Then came the thought of the sharks. A quick shiver shook me, and I gasped—which caused, more sea water to be added to the amount already in me.

I had always had a horror of sharks, and even in the swimming pool the mere thought of them always used to make me shudder involuntarily. Now that I was really among man eaters, and in danger of being attacked, I was almost in a frenzy. I peered about the surface of the water for fins, but there were none in sight. Taking heart, I increased my speed and determined to try to keep my self-control.

My clothing hindered me to some extent, but the absence of shoes was a great help. I thanked God fervently that I had removed them. The thought of the dagger at my side was encouraging, although I knew it was useless in this case. Nevertheless it was a moral support.

Looking backward, I could discover no fins; yet the darkened water had an ominous look, and every second was one of apprehension. I was all aquiver, half expecting to feel the shock of some brute's jaw at any moment.

The island was looming up at a greater rate than I had dared to hope. I figured that the tide was running with me, and at a very rapid rate; there was probably some narrow cut nearby in the chain of islands through which all the pent-up water had to flow, thus causing a tide race. I afterward discovered this was the case.

I wondered whether the sharks had followed the boat, or were on my scent. My scalp had been cut by the blow I had received, as I could tell by rubbing my fingers over my head. Doubtless it must have bled somewhat, and was probably still bleeding. Whether a shark could scent such a small amount of blood was questionable in my mind; however, I was not too optimistic, as I had heard stories of the trailing powers of sharks.

I hadn't the slightest idea how to fight a shark at night and in deep water. I had once had a theory on the subject, but now it seemed an absurd and fantastic idea. I kept swimming on.

For some time I had good luck; my occasional backward glances disclosed nothing disturbing. When I was getting near the island, and was already feeling thankful for my deliverance, the moon came from under the clouds and cast a remarkably bright light over the ocean.

Then I saw a sight that turned me sick. There, about a hundred yards behind me, was an object darting hither and thither through the water. A fin! I swam with all my speed; there was still hope, for I was near the island. But the blow on my head had taken more out of me than I had thought. I was growing tired rapidly. Then the fin disappeared again. This was even worse.

At any minute the shark might be upon me; I would have absolutely no warning. There would simply be a shock at some part of my body, and the race would be over. I was very tired and was fast losing my head. But I would fight it out; I would not give up till—

Something hit my leg a stunning blow. I practically fainted with fright and despair, and relaxed. The next moment my feet were touching bottom—hard and jagged. I had struck my leg against a piece of coral rock.

The water was about waist deep, so I began to wade swiftly toward the shore, now about a hundred and fifty yards away. I looked for the fin. There it was, about even with me, and some little distance to my left. I waded as quietly as I could, keeping my gaze on the fin. But the water began to get deeper, and was soon up to my neck. Not until then did I realize that I had been walking on a coral ledge. Looking toward the shore, and looking backward, I noticed that the water in front of me was a different color from that around me. It was over my depth between me and the island!

This was a disheartening discovery, for I had expected to be in water a little more than knee high within the next minute, and safe from the man eater. Now there was between me and safety over a hundred yards of deep water in which I would be lost if the shark got near me. In shallow water I had a chance.

If I only knew where the monster was I could decide what to do. I watched the surface intently; the fin appeared directly between me and the shore. It was a large one, and evidently its owner was not a sand shark. My only chance was to return to the reef, and I did so as fast as supreme fear could carry me.

When I got to water a little less than waist deep I stopped. I would stand there and rest, and hoped to escape notice by remaining absolutely still. If the beast scented or saw me, I would fight it out right there. I had a knife; it was dull, but long and heavy, and I was on my feet and could use it. Besides, I had an idea.

It was the plan of battle against sharks I had conceived several years earlier, as I had watched men "dive" turtles—turtles weighing hundreds of pounds and measuring five or six feet across the back. The men had seized both sides of the shell and had forced the beasts to come to the surface by tilting their bodies upward.

The fin was approaching me in a zigzag course. I could see the form of the shark now; this portion of the reef was white, and the dark shadow showed up clearly. I drew the knife out of its sheath and stood clutching it and shivering in the light breeze.

At last it caught sight of me, and darted through the water. In a second it was upon me. Pushing to the right, I struck at the great body as it flashed by. The knife did not penetrate the thick hide. One of my hopes had proved to be false. I quickly sheathed my weapon. It was up to me to use the other method, more dangerous and more fantastic, but now offering the best hope of escape.

The shark did not go far past me; with a quick bend of its head and body, and a furious swing of its tail, it was rushing toward me again. I waited, unable to breathe. I wanted terribly to run, or step to one side—but I stood fast till I could see the white of its belly as it turned on its side to strike. Then I plunged right across its track. The plunge was well timed, and I was out of danger, for the beast's mouth was on the side of its body away from me.

As I had expected, it followed me directly, swinging around with its back still toward me. Fortunately it could not turn sharply enough to bring its jaws toward me; so there we were within a foot or two of each other, and the shark unable to strike. I knew it would roll, and that would be the end of me, for then I would be directly in front of those terrible jaws.

With the greatest sense of abandonment I have ever experienced I threw myself upon the fish, just behind its head. To wrap my arms around its body was the work of a moment; then my legs were clamped about it in the wrestler's scissors hold. The skin I clung to was not slimy. I could keep my hold for a moment at least.

The tables were turned now—I was attacking the shark. It

trembled for just a fraction of a second, and then I seemed to cut through the water with the speed of a bullet. It was if the water had hands, and was clutching me by every square inch of my skin, attempting to drag me from the shark's back. But I stuck, for his skin was quite rough, and my leg muscles had been well trained for just such a crisis by four years of wrestling at college. My lungs were bursting—it seemed I had been under water for years.

Then we came to the surface for a second, and I breathed. The shark had changed its tactics—it was thrashing about in an effort to reach my legs with its mouth. It could not reach me.

Failing in its attempt to cut me in two, it began to roll. It spun over and over till my head was in a whirl; and then we dashed off under water again, not quite so-fast this time. Loosening up with my right arm, I moved my hand forward and up; round and round and back and forth I gently passed it, till I felt the soft spot I was seeking. Then with a vast repugnance I plunged my two fingers home.

The effect was instantaneous. We went in every direction at once. Withdrawing my hand, I clasped the shark with all my strength. We went straight up. The water broke from over my body, and I saw the surface several feet below me. Then we came down, with a crash and a shock. I was bent and twisted and battered—the furious brute lashed and jumped.

When I was all but exhausted we tore off again at a blinding speed through the tugging water. I advanced my hand and repeated my former actions. However, this time I did not remove my finger when the cyclone came, but in addition inserted my thumb and squeezed. I felt a "popping motion"—the only way I can describe the sensation—of the soft round thing in my hand. When I withdrew my hand this time it was not empty. I dropped the object, and my hand was back clinging on the shark's belly. As we broke through the surface this time I saw the island not more than twenty yards away.

When we crashed back into the water I was on the bottom and my opponent on top. Almost crushed, I rallied for the final move. Advancing my left hand, I sought the other eye. But before I found it I felt a pain in my side and then a ripping sensation as if I were being opened with a knife. The rocks! He was scraping me on the bottom! At that moment I found the eye. I made short work; but not before my clothes and half my skin had been shredded by the rocks and sand.

Unlocking my legs, I placed my feet against the brute's back; then withdrawing my hands, I gave myself a hearty send-off from my antagonist. The water was about three feet deep. In a moment I was on my feet, running madly for the mangroves just ahead. I could hear the frantic lashings of the wounded beast; he moved about in furious spurts, vainly seeking to close his teeth on me. In a moment I was safe. He was over twenty yards away, and could never in the world catch me without his eyesight. As I reached the trees growing in the water I saw my enemy turn, dash erratically away. I felt no pity for him. It had been too close a call.

I opened my left hand and regarded the torn eye I had involuntarily held during my dash. With a shudder of disgust I quickly threw it from me; then as quickly snatched it up again. I remembered that by boiling a fish's eyes, and then allowing the pupil to dry out slowly, a beautiful, pearl-like little ball was formed. I took a wet handkerchief from my pocket, carefully wrapped up the eye, and replaced the handkerchief. After washing my hands in the water, I turned to consider my predicament.

In front of me there was a tangled mass of roots rising from the water; above the roots huddled the trunks and branches of the mangrove trees. I knew that a great many of these coral islands were entirely covered by a foot or so of water at high tide; and I profoundly hoped that this one was different. The only way to find out was to do a bit of exploring, so I waded forward and clambered up on the first roots I encountered.

As I reached the branches I heard a flapping noise, and

something struck me in the face. Then came a hoarse croak; the next moment the air fairly hummed with a great whirring noise, accompanied by startled cries. I had crawled right into a rookery of some kind of birds.

It was quite dark in the shadow of the dense foliage. After crawling monkey-fashion for some time over the arching roots and spreading branches I gave up the search for dry land. As far as I went there was water beneath me, and I was forced to come to the unpleasant conclusion that I was on a submerged island. I might find ground not actually covered by water, but it would have been soggy and alive with crabs and perhaps reptiles.

I made my way back to the shore, determined to sleep among the branches. At last I found what I was seeking—the limbs of several trees interlaced and woven like a piece of gigantic basket work, forming a sort of concave. Small branches had grown between and quite a substantial fabric was the result. I broke many more branches and placed them over this frame, till at last I had a rather decent bed. When I had improved it to the limit of my resources I lay down and wriggled into as comfortable a position as possible.

CHAPTER IV

A STARTLING DISCOVERY

MY BED WAS far from soft, and sleep was long in coming. The boughs pressed hard against my body, and it was necessary to shift position frequently; which I had to do very carefully because of my bruised ribs. However, at length my discomfort proved to be less than my weariness, and I sank into a doze.

Various episodes of the day flitted through my fevered brain—things distorted and ludicrous. I saw Dr. Grame before me; and when I approached to ask him what time it was, he suddenly changed to a shark and rushed away in search of his eyes. I dreamed of many other things, some intelligible, some confused and cloudy. Only one is worth being related.

I thought I was lying in my berth on the Mermaid, half asleep. Suddenly I was aware of something peering into my face. It was Nicky. Strangely enough, he was hanging from the ceiling. I waited, but he only swung gently to and fro and leered. He did not look natural—there was a change, but I could not determine the nature of it; the features were his, but exaggerated, as in a caricature.

The hanging, grinning face was extremely annoying, and I kicked at it wildly. The first time I missed my mark, but the second kick went home with telling force. The body fell; then he suddenly grabbed my foot, and I felt a sharp pain in my toe. He had bitten me. I began kicking at him wildly, and he disappeared into the gloom; but he was not walking; it was as if he were pulling himself through the air hand over hand, like a sailor climbing rope.

The vividness of my dream awakened me, but, after twisting my aching body into a better position, I soon fell asleep again. When next I awoke it was broad daylight. My side was very stiff and somewhat painful. A short inspection told me the injuries would not be dangerous if they did not become infected.

Feeling a pain in my foot, I bent forward stiffly; to my utter bewilderment, there were three little holes in my large toe. I remembered my dream of the night before; but dreams do not bite, and I was at a loss to account for the wound—unless, perhaps, it had been made by the sharp coral rocks, which I doubted greatly. My attention, however, was soon diverted from my toe by thirst and hunger, so I started for the shore to take stock of my position.

When I arrived at the water, I stripped and swam out to the mud flat to get a general view of my island. It was long and low, but seemed to have a slight rise in the center; this probably meant dry ground, so I determined to penetrate to this higher position as soon as I had finished my observations.

At some distance away to the right were several large islands, seemingly much more above the water level than my present refuge—which I had dubbed to myself as "Devil's Island"—having in mind my toe. I made a mental note that at the first opportunity I would attempt a passage to these islands, as they would be healthier and offered a possibility of finding fresh water.

The morning was still cool—I judged it must have been around nine o'clock. Before me I could see nothing but the green mangrove trees, twisting their roots in every direction and casting deep shadows over the black water. It was not a reassuring thought that I would have to find my living for some time to come in this mess of mud, roots, and branches.

As I approached the island, intent on, getting to the interior without delay, two dark-colored wisps protruding from a rock pocket caught my attention. There was no current, and yet they were moving. Crawfish! Although I had no means of making a fire, I realized the advantage of having something to eat, even if it must be eaten raw.

Reaching down I gently poked the feelers with one hand. As the body slowly appeared, I seized it with the other. It flapped its tail and resisted violently; I felt it pushing on my hand with its legs in a vain effort to escape. I lifted it, and with a twist, separated the tail from the carcass, which I tossed aside into the water. I deposited the retained part, where the only edible meat is located, in my pocket when I reached my clothes, and began to crawl inland from tree to tree.

After I had made my way for some time in this laborious fashion, the ground became hard enough to walk on, and I resumed a normal method of advance. The footing steadily got firmer, and the mangroves gave way to a sort of heavy sedge grass. At last I arrived at an opening, in the middle of which I saw, to my joy, several stunted palms, laden with coconuts. Here, at any rate, was something to drink. Dragging one of the green coconuts from its stem, I proceeded to pound it on a rock to get the outer husk off. Some fifteen minutes of such treatment brought success. The nut was now in the condition in which we find it in grocery stores; so the next problem was to pierce one of the three eyes, and get at the liquid inside. I accomplished this by means of a thin splinter of rock, and the next minute I experienced the joy of slaking a deep thirst.

After all the milk was gone I broke the shell, and put the meat into my pocket after eating not a little. The coconut trees were a great discovery. Here were food and drink for several days at least, and there were probably more trees scattered about.

Landmarks are most helpful in any strange place, so in order to distinguish this clearing from any other I might run across later, I decided to erect a little mound of stones. As I was kicking about in the grass in search of building materials, something white caught my attention.

When I pushed away the sticks and grass, there lay in front of me a human skeleton. I was startled and somewhat upset, as may be imagined. One fact about the thing struck me as being peculiar—the man must have had tremendous depth and breadth of chest. I wondered even then at the power those muscles must have had. Yet how little good had it done him!

It was hard not to be discouraged by the sight of such a sinister omen of the future; so I left the opening, with its palms and bleached bones, and continued my exploring.

For several hours I trudged about, but found no more high land, and consequently no more palm trees. The number of spiders in the mangrove trees surprised me—the things were perfectly enormous, with long, hairy legs. It was a lucky thing I had not seen them the night before, or I might have slept even less than I did. On the marshy ground, myriads of crabs of all descriptions scurried to and fro, ducking swiftly into their holes at my approach. I encountered no snakes, for which I was very thankful.

Directing my way in as much of a straight line as possible, at length I arrived at the other side of the island. The general appearance was much the same as that of the side on which I had landed. However, here and there among the mangroves, I saw planks.

Though old and somewhat water-logged, they cheered me up; at least they were once a part of civilization. Thinking that I might be able to construct a raft from them, or use them in erecting a shelter, I spent quite a long time in herding as many as I could find into a little cove in the mangroves, where there would be no possibility of their being washed away.

While I worked the sun went under the clouds; also it seemed to me as if the wind was freshening. By the time I had collected all the planks in sight, it was blowing almost a gale, with the waves splashing through the tangle of roots, and the branches swishing about viciously. It was getting chilly, so I determined to return to the palm trees, which I had established as my headquarters. Before leaving I crawled out among the trees to have a look at the ocean and the sky.

The clouds were inky-black, and sweeping across the sky at an astounding rate. The waves were capped with white, and were beginning to assume large proportions. The noise of them breaking on the coral reef in front was like a continuous peal of thunder. There was little doubt that it would be a wild night, and I was thankful for the high ground.

Shortly after I arrived at the palm clearing, it began to rain. It was a cutting rain, for the wind drove the water down at a fierce slant. I placed whatever stones and rubbish I could find at the foot of the largest of the palms; this afforded a partial shelter from the wind, making things much more comfortable. Although it could not have been much after four o'clock in the afternoon, it was almost as dark as night.

I knew I would be unable to accomplish anything until the next day, so, as I was very tired, and had not had much sleep the preceding night, I curled up and closed my eyes.

This was the first moment since I had left the Mermaid that my mind had not been occupied; and for the first time I gave myself up to reflections. I tried to imagine who it could have been that had pushed me overboard. What could have been the motive? My mind became confused from trying to pin suspicion on the most likely person, and I turned to wondering what they were doing on the boat.

When I had been found missing they certainly had put about and retraced their course. The probability was that my absence had not been discovered till the morning after my accident. What had Eleanor done when she learned of my disappearance? Had she merely felt sympathy for a fellow traveler who had possibly been drowned, or had she felt deeper emotion? There was no way of knowing such things; so I contented myself with reviewing the course of our friendship.

Then my thoughts wandered to Nicky. What a peculiar mixture of sweetness and brutality he was! I could not free my mind of the picture of his wrinkled little face. And Dr. Grame, as picturesque in his generation as Nicky was in his, I could imagine him a hardy old Viking: a blustering, hard-hitting man-driver, who could live up to his bluster. My recollections gradually became more and more confused and indistinct, and before long I was asleep.

Several times during the night I was awakened by the fury of the storm. The rain had stopped, but the wind blew more fiercely than ever. The thunder of the distant waves, and the shrieking of the wind through the mangroves blended into a pulsing roar. Once, when I awakened, the moon was out, and the palm tree above me did not seem to be bending to such an acute angle as formerly. However, the skies were still lowering, and the wind still furious.

I awoke again at daylight. The storm had died down, and only the roar of the waves remained. The sun was out at intervals, and a stiff breeze set the leaves of the palms to rustling and clacking out their quaint melody.

My first labor was to shell a coconut. After this had been accomplished, and I had had my breakfast, I set out for the cove into which I had gathered planks the night before. The wind was blowing toward the group of islands I had determined to visit. If I could get a raft constructed in a couple of hours, I could use my clothing as a sail, and escape a long paddle.

As I hurried through the roots and branches it struck me that nature was particularly cheerful this day. The leaves were a fresh green, and the sky had a clean, sunny look. The land crabs raced merrily to their holes at my approach, and there were not as many spiders to be seen as usual.

Withal I was happy; I had eaten, and drunk, and my soreness was fast leaving me. Although I had seen no traces of the Mermaid as yet there was no doubt that my friends would look for me until I was found. I did not expect to see the boat for a day or so, as the storm very probably had forced them to anchor in the lee of some island.

I was overjoyed to find all my planks undisturbed, for I had feared they might have been washed away by the violence of the waves. I started to work immediately, for I didn't care to run the risk of having the wind change direction before I was ready to set sail for the group of large islands.

Although several of the planks were full of nails, I determined to use as few as possible, and save the rest for future needs. Extracting the rusty things was hard work, but the big knife came in handy, and at last I had them all out. Most of them were almost rusted away, but some still seemed to have considerable strength. Now the work of construction was ready, but before beginning I felt inclined to rest a moment; so I climbed to the outmost mangrove roots to have a look at the ocean, in hopes that I might catch sight of the Mermaid.

It would not be correct to say that I was disappointed, for I had not expected any such luck; but at all events the Mermaid was not in sight. However, there was something being tossed about by the waves a quarter of a mile or so out that attracted my attention.

I could not see it distinctly, but it looked as if it might possibly have been a human form on a half submerged raft. I strained my eyes for several minutes. I could make out no details, but my conviction grew that the thing was a raft with some one—or something—on it.

The only way to find out was to swim out and see. Thoughts of sharks caused me to hesitate, but I decided quite sanely that the probability of there being any sharks about was small, as they take to deeper water in cold, rough weather. Moreover, there were no sawfish remains at hand to attract them from their usual feeding grounds.

I struck out, having left the greater part of my clothes in a tree. Even if it turned out that there was no one on the floating object which so resembled a raft, there might be something on it that would prove useful to me. And even if the latter supposition should prove to be untrue I should at least have the raft.

As I drew nearer the raft became visible every time I was lifted by a wave. Before long it was apparent that the object on the raft was a human body. Spurred on by this verification of my guess, I fairly tore through the water. When I was no more than fifty yards away I saw it was a girl. It seemed as if I should never cover the intervening distance. However, I finally did reach the raft, and clung to it while deciding what to do. The girl's head was partly submerged in the water; in order to make sure she would not be drowned I turned the body over. It was Eleanor!

CHAPTER V

GONE!

YOU CAN IMAGINE my surprise. Nor was my anxiety less. The body did not show any indications of death. Placing my hand over her heart I found it was still beating, and thanked heaven.

The return was slow work. Pushing the raft ahead of me, I came at last to shallow water. I took Eleanor in my arms, and walked to the mangroves, pushing the raft along also. Even in my surprise I did not forget that. Scrambling over the roots to dry land was a task; I slipped several times, and almost dropped my burden before I finally came to a firm footing.

As I held Eleanor in my arms I could feel her breathing. I judged she did not have any quantity of water in her lungs, but was merely unconscious. Calling and shaking her were of no avail; she stirred a little, but did not open her eyes. The tree in which I had left my clothing was nearby, so I stumbled to it. There was no place to put Eleanor while I donned my apparel, so I draped it over my shoulders, and set out for the clearing.

With her head pillowed against my left shoulder, and her face tilted toward the sky, Eleanor breathed regularly. Furthermore, her color was as rosy as it had ever been, hence my anxiety about her was forgotten. She would come to before long, no doubt, and would be none the worse for her adventure.

The world was bright again, even the crawling things that trundled away at our approach seemed beautiful. A buzzard passing overhead seemed a softer black, and the smell of decaying seaweed was less repulsive than formerly.

When I looked at the helpless little face so near mine, with its clustering bobbed hair, fine eyebrows, and enticing, but strong, mouth, I flushed and turned my eyes away, as was fitting. But instead of being strong and keeping my attention fixed on my path, I looked at Eleanor again. As a rule I do not give way to impulses, but this time I very caddishly planted a kiss full on those parted lips.

I ought to have felt very miserable and conscious-stricken, but I cannot even boast penitence. Being only a man, and therefore a fool, I found the audacity to let my regard wander back to the unconscious face again. There, looking directly at me, were two wide-open eyes. An expression of surprise—perhaps even amusement—flickered there a moment, and then the eyes closed. I called her name and resorted to all the arts of reviving the unconscious, but to no avail. Then bethinking myself of the success of my unconventional method used a moment before, I applied the same treatment again, but with no result.

I carefully deposited Eleanor on the first dry spot we came to, and hurriedly crawled into a few more of my garments. When I considered I made a fairly respectable appearance, I took up the unconscious girl again and stumbled on to the clearing.

Once more "home," I put Eleanor on a bed of palm fiber that I had collected the day before, and placed my coat under her head as a pillow. Then thinking she would probably be hungry when she awoke, I began extracting a coconut from its tough covering. The noise evidently roused Eleanor, for when I turned toward her with the nut, her eyes were open. She regarded me in a vague, puzzled way.

Being at loss what to say, I offered her the coconut. She drank deeply, and then laughed.

"Well, this is a pretty mess, isn't it? What happened to *you?*"

"Oh, I got hit over the head and tossed overboard. But how did *you* happen to get here?"

With a little shudder she told me how the Mermaid had run on a reef, and how the waves had battered the boat against the rocks. The captain had said that the only way of escape lay in the small boats. All had equipped themselves with life preservers, revolvers, water-tight match boxes, etc.

In the melee of launching the lifeboats, Eleanor had slipped, and plunged into the water. She had seen the young underengineer Don dive in after her, but he did not reach her. Tossed and ducked by the fierce, driving waves, she had finally found herself beside the raft. Where it had come from she did not know. Hour after hour had been spent in clinging to its tossing surface.

Through the dark night, burning with thirst and battered by the waves, she had borne up. At last she had fallen asleep—and when she came to, she had seen me.

In my turn, I told her of my adventure; the mysterious blow, the fight with the shark. Devil's Island, and my discovery of her.

From a pocket of her dress she triumphantly produced a match box and a revolver. We could only afford to use one match, so the hunting knife was worked a long time cutting fine slivers from dead branches. A quantity of dry sedge grass was added, and there was no trouble at all in starting a roaring fire. Now that we had a means of cooking food, I thought of the multitude of fish and crawfish that were within our reach, and determined to lunch on fish that very noon. Eleanor was lying on the bed, apparently tired out.

"How'd you like some roast fish?" I inquired.

"Splendid," she said gayly. "I think I could eat several."

"I'm going down to try to catch some."

"I want to go along, of course," she said.

I firmly refused to be accompanied, and Eleanor reluctantly agreed to remain by the fire and dry out her clothes. As I left

I told her to call out if she wanted me; the shore was within easy hailing distance.

Catching fish with the bare hands was not as easy as I had imagined. Finally I managed to corner a large mangrove snapper, and was able to seize him as he struggled in vain, to push between a couple of roots. Holding a fish is even harder than catching one, and I was not sure of my prize till its head was amputated. In a half hour more I had captured another fish, as well as several crawfish. Satisfied with my catch, I returned to the clearing.

Eleanor shouted at me on my approach, and ran to meet me.

"My, you are quite a hunter, aren't you?"

"Fisherman, Ellie."

"Anything you want to call it," she said. "Oh, aren't they awful?"—pointing at the crawfish. "Did you really catch them with your hands? I should be frightened to death to touch one," she babbled. "But I'll do it anyway."

She put out one slender finger gingerly and barely touched the rough shell. "There, I *am* brave, am I not?" she asked in a tone demanding an affirmative answer.

Roasting the fish was a delicate job. We ran long twigs through small pieces at a time, and turned them slowly, as one sees fowls being roasted on a spit in a rotisserie. It was hot work, and more than one piece was badly burned. But we were ravenously hungry, so the ill-cooked morsels tasted like ambrosia. I had eaten nothing but coconuts since I left the boat two nights before; you can guess how much I enjoyed the meal.

Eleanor felt quite strong after having eaten, and volunteered to help me with the raft. We piled up a great quantity of dry wood on the fire, and then threw on green foliage. The result was a large column of heavy gray smoke, which mounted up and up.

"If they can't see that, they are blind," I muttered as the finishing touches were added.

I heard a little cough, and felt Eleanor grasp my arm. She

was trying hard not to cry, but the corners of her mouth were twitching.

"Jimmy," she cried pitifully, "I can't help wondering what happened to them. What if their boats were smashed on the reef?"

I belittled the danger to her family—scoffing at the idea. I assured her there could not possibly have been any accident, and that they were safely landed on some nearby island at that very moment.

Whether she believed me or not, I do not know. At all events my confidence cheered her up, and to all appearances she gave no more thought to any danger as far as her family were concerned.

Sunset saw the completion of our craft. It consisted of the raft that had borne Eleanor, considerably bolstered up and strengthened by the addition of all my boards. It was really a very good raft with its deck a foot or so above the level of the water, and no possibility of capsizing. Besides, it was equipped with a mast, which would be most useful if the wind held out in the same quarter. While I labored on our ship, Eleanor trapped fish. Six good sized snappers told the story of her efforts.

That night we had another fish roast. It really was quite jolly, sitting near the fire and chatting intimately. There we were, isolated from society, with no conveniences, and in more or less danger, still taking life as calmly as if we had been sitting on the top of a Fifth Avenue bus.

The sky above was almost cloudless—now and then a bit of fleece would be whisked across the moon, and assume a momentary brilliance, only to fade back to a dull gray again. The stars were bright and numerous; it was just cool enough to be pleasant, and, above all, there were no mosquitoes. Although castaways, we were in a contented frame of mind. There was no real danger; we would find the survivors of the Mermaid in a day or so, and all be picked up by a passing yacht or schooner within a week.

It sounds odd, but we actually discussed the stage hits of the season. Musical comedies, dramas, and farces all received our impartial attention. Then we branched off into literature, and gave much thought to Robinson Crusoe.

"Our adventure would be perfect, Jimmy, if we could capture a wild man and take him home with us," said Eleanor.

"Fine, as long as some of us did not go into the family stew pot," I could not help remarking. "However, I don't believe anything larger than a land crab exists in any of these islands around here. Thank Heaven for that. I have no inclinations for standing guard at night."

"Standing guard is exciting," she burst out. "I stood guard once—with a loaded shot gun. It was at camp; we had heard some one climbing the ladder into a loft at night, and wandering around the storeroom upstairs. One night we sneaked in with our bedding, and took turns watching the door, shotgun in hand. Toward morning we heard the rungs of the ladder creaking—my heart nearly stopped beating. It turned out to be the cat, and my adventure was spoiled."

"What would you have done if it had been a man?" I asked.

"Screamed, I suppose," she admitted with a laugh.

"Would you have shot him?" I demanded.

Eleanor reflected a moment. The firelight played on the regular features under her tousled hair. "I'm afraid I could have if it had been necessary—only I would never have gotten over it," she admitted at last.

"Well, there won't be any need for killing on this expedition," I confidently assured her.

She looked into the fire, and shivered as the squawk of some night bird floated to us, as if in answer.

"I hope not," she murmured. "But aren't we getting a bit dismal?" she added, with a bright smile.

"We are, unnecessarily," I answered. "Guess we had better

get a little sleep pretty soon. You must be fagged out; and we'll want to get an early start to-morrow."

"All right, I *am* pretty tired. Where shall I sleep?"

This was a question. After some discussion, we decided I should go down to the raft and pull a couple of boards from it. From these and some of the coconut fiber, a small shelter could be constructed at the foot of one of the trees. Eleanor could sleep here, and I would sleep some twenty feet away, by the fire.

"It's too bad we can't live up to the story book traditions, and each take possession of one-half of the island; but I think in the circumstances it would be running unnecessary danger to stay very far away from each other."

"This is much more congenial, anyway," laughed Eleanor.

I had to make my way to the raft very slowly because the ground was rough, and I had no shoes. I stumbled several times, and stubbed my toe cruelly. However, I finally reached the shore, a little above the raft.

As I was looking about in an attempt to locate it, I heard a crackling of twigs. Peering in the direction from which the sound came, I could see nothing. I was about to walk on, thinking it was an extra large crab, when the sound was repeated, louder this time. Wondering what would be moving about at this time of night, I shrank back into the shadows and waited. The crackling kept up; it was accompanied by a swishing noise, which had not been audible before. Whatever was causing the disturbance among the twigs and branches was evidently coming directly toward my place of concealment.

I was beginning to get a bit excited, for my ears told me that it was something of considerable bulk. And then I caught sight of it; a large, dark body appearing for a moment between the trunks and leaves, and then disappearing again. What was it? I hadn't the slightest idea, as my glimpse had been fleeting, and was blurred by the branches.

It seemed to me the thing was working inland. I thought of Eleanor, and forgot the planks. Moving as quietly as possible,

I started back for the clearing. The beast had turned off obliquely toward the right, and the further away from the coast I went, the more we were divided. Nevertheless, I drew my knife, and advanced with it in my hand.

When I was within several paces of the clearing, I threw off my stealth, and came stumping up to the fire.

When Eleanor saw me empty handed, she threw me a glance of inquiry.

"I couldn't get any planks loose," I lied, "besides, I think it would be better if we both slept near, the fire. It's going to be pretty cold to-night. You can have that side, and I'll take this one."

Eleanor laughed indulgently.

"I believe you're lazy, that's all," she said. Then compassionately, "It was a shame to send you down there without any shoes. We'll have to find you something for a substitute."

We dragged the fiber over to the fire, and made a pallet on each side. After finishing this, and having looked around, I asked:

"Let's have a look at your gun, Ellie. Got any cartridges?"

She produced both, and I surprised her very much by cleaning up the gun with a piece of my shirt, and testing its action.

Before we finally lay down to catch a little sleep, I gave her the revolver and remarked:

"Better keep it at hand—it won't do any harm, and you love adventure."

I lay on my side till I knew by Eleanor's heavy breathing that she was asleep; then I rose to a sitting position, and began my long watch.

MY HEAD throbbed stormily; the only sound was the rustling of the chill breeze in the fans of the palm trees. I tried to think; the Mermaid—sharks—crawfish. My thoughts would not coordinate—I must have sunk into unconsciousness.

Suddenly I sat up with a start. The cool, silent day was just breaking in the east, casting a gold and brown light on the clouds that brooded over the dim expanse of sea and reef. My head was not aching so violently now, and it all came back to me.

I looked across the dead ashes of the fire, and saw only a tangled pallet of coconut fiber. Eleanor was no longer there! Running my hand over my head, I felt a large lump under the blood matted hair. Then the thought that had for some time been lurking in the back of my brain found expression; I had been clubbed, and my companion had been carried away!

CHAPTER VI

A DREAD SUSPICION

MY FIRST REACTION was amazement and incredulity. I could not realize that anything had happened. However, the empty pallet before me was a clamorous proof that Eleanor was not where she should have been, and the ache in my head told me that I had been dealt a heavy blow.

As I rose to my feet a rapid fire of questions ran through my mind. What had struck me on the head? What had become of Eleanor? Was she nearby or far away? A hasty survey of the clearing disclosed no signs of the missing girl. Everything, except the tumbled and wrecked pallet, was just as it had been the night before.

Lifting my voice, I called Eleanor's name loudly. The mass of waving green mangroves seemed to devour the sound, for no echo came back, and the stillness was even greater than before.

After shouting for several minutes without a response, I flung myself down on the ground and fell to reviling myself for having fallen asleep at my post. Eleanor had been in my care, and I had betrayed my trust. If I had only stayed awake!

Action, the natural reaction of remorse, brought me to my feet again. A thorough search of the island, which lasted till long after sunrise, produced no results.

Something, or some one, had hit me on the head while I slept; the same thing must have carried Eleanor away. The thought of the mysterious object I had seen moving through the trees the night before kept returning to my mind. Could it have been a man?

The memory of my bitten toe and the dream connected with it came to my thoughts more than once. At last I determined to give up conjecturing as to what had happened, and turn my entire attention to recovering Eleanor.

Of one thing I was practically certain: Eleanor was not on Devil's Island. Therefore, she was either dead and in the ocean, or had been taken to the group of islands I had noticed before.

As I saw it now, there was only one course to pursue—to make one more tour of the island and then head my raft for the keys to the west.

So I sat down and hurriedly bolted some of the roast fish that remained from our supper of the night before. I realized that I must eat to provide the strength I would surely need for the day that lay ahead of me.

When I had finished my scant meal, I turned my attention to Eleanor's bed, which showed every sign that a struggle had taken place on it. Making a careful search, I found the revolver and cartridge belt under the pile of palm fiber; a discovery which, needless to say, filled me with the greatest joy. For many things are possible to an armed man that would be hopeless for one with empty hands.

To be quite frank, I was afraid to think of the danger Eleanor might be in. I had done enough thinking; it was time for action now. Making one more rapid tour of the island, I came to our raft, and at last embarked on the run I had been contemplating ever since my arrival at this island of surprises.

My shirt turned out to be an admirable sail. The wind was slight, but the raft slid smoothly along with the waves sloshing against its sides. To be absolutely alone is a disquieting feeling. As I looked into the dark depths of the water all about me, I shivered. Who knew what might not exist down there? My imagination painted pictures of sharks of unheard-of lengths, with ravenous appetites. The serpents of nursery tales did not seem at all improbable now.

I sat as nearly in the middle of the raft as possible, in order to be at the greatest distance from the water. How I craved a companion! If Eleanor had been with me, I would have been the happiest man in the world. The day was just warm enough to be pleasant, and the salty tang of the sea could not efface the balminess of the breeze.

As I said before, the raft was really making very good progress. We were getting nearer and nearer to the group of islands. It was evident that they were of quite different nature from the one I had left Although part of the shore line was overhung with mangroves, yet there were long stretches of sandy beach to be seen.

The interior of the islands seemed to be from thirty to forty feet above the level of the sea. Instead of the marshy, mangrove-covered Devil's Island, I knew enough to expect a dense forest of tropical trees—almost a jungle. Here would be animal life. I wondered whether such a place would be very safe. At all events, it would be far more comfortable than on the lower islands.

If my guess was correct, Eleanor was on one of these islands.

On the whole, my chances of rescuing her were very good. I was armed with a revolver and about fifty cartridges. If I could not render a good account of myself under such conditions, I would indeed be a poor excuse for a man.

My gaze wandered incessantly from island to island, from cove to cove. There ought to be some visible signs that would hint at her whereabouts. And my guess was not incorrect. In the sky above the largest of the keys was a dirty streak which looked very much like smoke. Using a loose board as a rudder, I began to steer the raft, since the wind was not blowing in quite the direction I wished to go. Luckily I was sufficiently versed in the ways of sailing to know that I would have to head above the desired spot, since we would make a great deal of leeway.

The sun hung above the rim of the ocean; before long it would be dark. By this time the smudge could definitely be made out as smoke. My excitement may be imagined. Somewhere on that island was Eleanor, with Heaven knew whom. It was my task to get her under my protection again. Goodness knows, it had been of little enough avail on Devil's Island; but I was determined that if I found her once more I would not lose her again.

There was one point that gave me not a little concern. Suppose I had been seen from the island? If I had, and my enemy were armed, it would be the easiest thing in the world for him to lie among the bushes on the shore and shoot me dead as I landed. On the other hand, he might take Eleanor and move quietly to another island. I wondered how conspicuous my raft and I were from the shore. There was no doubt that we had been seen if any one had been watching the ocean carefully.

After thinking the matter over for a considerable time, I chose a plan that seemed to meet all the exigencies of the situation. There was a small island some three or four hundred yards from the larger one. If I could reach this island unseen, it would be very easy to swim to my destination in the twilight, at which time I would be hardly visible.

If I should slide into the water now, and cling to the end of the raft, I would be absolutely invisible from land. I followed out the plan immediately, first laying the pistol, cartridges and match case on the raft. Then I clung to the rear edge and aided the sail by kicking with my feet; but I was careful to keep in the cool brine to avoid splashing. Even if any one should see the raft, he would see nothing on it, and conclude it to be a derelict floating about.

My fear of the depths below left me when I was actually in the water. Besides, I had more important things to think of. Eleanor was somewhere in that jungle, doubtless in danger. What time had I to conjure up nameless terrors of the sea?

The rest of the journey to the small island was without event. I chose a small bay into which to guide the raft. Knowing that I might have future need of this primitive boat, I pulled it in among the roots of the mangroves. I was not satisfied to leave it until it was so thoroughly entangled that there was no chance of it floating away with the tide.

Before setting out to reconnoiter the large island, I paused to observe the general lay of the land. Through the branches of the mangroves could be seen a long white beach that stretched to my right—away from Large Island, as I called it.

To the left nothing was visible but twisting trees. In the opposite direction from Large Island was another key, with a great crescent-shaped shore line. In my own mind I named this Crescent Island.

As I was admiring the long stretch of white beach I was given cause for surprise. For there curling above the top of the foliage was an unmistakable wisp of smoke. My gaze was glued on it for some time. There was no mistaking it. There was a fire on this island too! Perhaps this stream of vapor was the real clue to Eleanor's whereabouts. It was difficult to decide which island should be visited first. However, I decided upon Large

Island, for no other reason than that it was the first one I had seen. I determined that if nothing turned up there I would return immediately to Crescent Island.

The sun was on the point of setting, but I could count on long twilight. I set out along the coast toward Large Island, which was not visible from my side of Small Island.

Traveling through the mangroves was slow work; so I gave up the land and swam across the narrow channel that skirted the shore. Separated from the island by deep water was a shallow bar which ran parallel to the coast. The water was about knee-deep, and I was able to make very good progress. The bar was evidently part of a coral reef, for the bottom was rocky and uneven, scarred with pockets from which protruded many cray-fish antennae. As I had no other food with me than a piece of coconut and a bit of cooked fish, I set about the capture of a couple of these tropical lobsters. Having pocketed the results of my foraging operations, I continued my way.

Ahead of me was a small promontory. I judged that this was the end of the island, and Large Island would soon be visible. As I drew near I noticed something in the water a little to my left.

It was a dark-brown object, and at first sight appeared to be a shark. It did not move, but bobbed up and down as the ripples rolled against it. I was too curious to pass it up without an investigation; and, as it looked perfectly harmless, approached it, but with great caution and with a loaded gun in my hand.

When I drew nearer I saw that it was a large, hairy body, no doubt drowned. My imagination was fired, and I raced toward it, forgetting all thoughts of my previous weariness. I stumbled once in a rock pocket, and narrowly escaped dousing the pistol. Cooled off by my accident, I continued more calmly.

The sight I saw on reaching the object was fearful. It was a large monkey, bloated and extended. I judged it had been dead a couple of days. As I wondered what had been the cause of its death, I noticed something near its head. I leaned over and looked more closely.

There, with its jaws clamped into the monkey's arm, was what seemed to be an enormous eel. Its body must have been from eight to ten inches through. I knew what it was. A moray! I had heard of them before, and had even caught a small one on a hook and line once. They are salt water eels, with massive jaws and long teeth that slant back toward the throat. If they once get their teeth into anything—so it is said—they cannot let go, because of the back-slanting teeth. At any rate, whether they can or whether they can't, they *don't* let go.

I had often heard stories of their seizing the foot of some poor fisherman who unwittingly trod upon them, and holding fast till the tide had risen, and the fisherman had drowned. I had never believed these stories, but here was proof. Only about two feet of the moray was outside his rock pocket; the rest of his body was on the inside. It would have taken a team of horses to move the thing.

They have a peculiar habit of tying their bodies into all kinds of knots. I knew this, because I saw it done by the small one I once captured. Whether they tie themselves into a knot around a rock inside their hole, I do not know. However, it is impossible to get them out.

The skin and surface flesh of the moray was in shreds. The ape had evidently put up a good fight, for the moray too was dead. I conjectured that the monkey had reached his arm into the rock pocket after a crayfish, and had disturbed the moray. The huge eel had seized the arm and pulled the ape under. The ape had drowned, but while doing so had inflicted such punishment on the moray that it could not survive.

It is needless to say that I decided to make the rest of my journey over the mangrove roots. I made my way cautiously to the shore, my mind full of tales of the ferocity of the salt water eel—how it will attack a boat if hooked; how poisonous its teeth are; that you have to break its back in three places to kill it, and so on. After I had reached the shore it was only a matter of a few minutes before I had come to the cape, and Large Island lay about two hundred yards away beyond a cut.

The smoke was still visible. It was impossible to say from what part of the island it was rising, but I judged the fire must be somewhere near the opposite shore.

Before letting myself into the water to begin the swim—I was in the mangrove branches, and the water below was over my head—I thought of the cartridges. Would they fire if wet? If the powder got damp, it was certain that they would not.

I did not know how water-tight the cases were, and was determined to run no more risks than necessary. I unfastened the cartridge belt, which I had been carrying around my neck when I encountered the moray and the dead monkey. Rolling it up as tightly as I could, I tied it with my handkerchief. Then I tore some strips from my shirt, and bound the rolled cartridge belt firmly to my head. When I was satisfied that it would not slip, I let myself down into the chilly water and set out for the other island.

The course of one's thoughts while swimming is curious indeed. I could not keep my attention on any one thing more than a moment at a time. My first thought was the possibility of the presence of sharks. Since my narrow escape it was always the first thing to come into my mind on entering the water. However, there was no particular reason why there should be any sharks in this cut, and if there were it was probable that they were only sand sharks. So I hoped for the best and continued on my way.

But what about the monkey? I had suspected their presence back on Devil's Island. The skeleton, the thing I saw while prowling around the night of Eleanor's disappearance, and the dream about Nicky biting my toe, all combined as significant in my mind. The marks of the bite had been visible the next morning. It was probably a little ape that had bitten me, and in my half conscious, half feverish condition I had dreamed it was Nicky. Then a terrible thought assailed me. Was it the apes who had stolen Eleanor?

Before long I was at the sandy beach, unstrapping the belt from my head. Somewhere before me, in the fast falling night, was Eleanor or a band of apes, or Heaven knows what!

CHAPTER VII

FRIENDS

LUCKILY FOR ME, tropical twilight was long at that time of year. I started off through the mangroves at as rapid a pace as possible. I had a general idea of the direction of the fire, and trusted to Providence to help me locate it.

Large Island was similar to Devil's Island, except the ground became higher and firmer more quickly. The undergrowth was dense; sand crabs were less numerous. The possibility of running across dangerous animals was not so remote, so I advanced with my pistol loaded and in my hand. However, I encountered no trouble.

Noises were audible on all sides, but I actually saw nothing except a small snake, which slid into the shadows as I approached. It was getting darker, and consequently more difficult to make rapid headway. After I covered about a mile, or what I thought was a mile, I began to wonder how much farther it was to the shore. It was almost dark, so I determined to climb a very tall tree which was nearby, while I could still see.

Climbing up was no easy matter; it cost me two barked shins, and not a little time and hard work. But when I did arrive at the topmost branches my pains were rewarded. Only a few hundred yards away the sea stretched out darkly, and a little distance down the coast I could see a column of smoke swirling up from behind a mass of trees and foliage.

My descent was rapid, and I was soon on my way again. Now that I knew where I was going, I picked my way carefully and tried to avoid making noise. It was quite dark except for the faint light of the stars. Luckily I had a smattering knowledge of astronomy, picked up in the classroom at college, and was able to direct my steps with some accuracy, allowing the heavenly bodies to point the way. It was slow going. Time after time I bumped slowly into the trunk of a tree, and becoming entangled in vines and bushes was a matter of every other minute. But I pursued my way doggedly, as I had a definite goal ahead of me. At last a dim red glare was visible through the trees. There, I knew, was the fire. Who were around it?

I advanced now with even greater caution. I seemed hardly to be moving at all, so great was my desire not to give myself away by any noise. At last the fire was visible, only to be blotted out the next moment by intervening foliage. But it came in sight again, and this time I could see the whole fire. As I drew nearer figures began to be visible; at first mere shadowy, shapeless bulks, moving here and there.

By this time I was on the edge of the hammock; ahead of me was sandy soil covered by a growth of thick, high grass. As I came nearer and nearer I was certain the forms moving about the fire were humans. I knew I had to come close enough to see the men's faces and hear their conversation. It was necessary to determine whether they were friends or enemies.

I crawled nearer and nearer, coming to within fifty feet of the fire. A low murmur of voices was audible, but the words themselves were lost. There were five people, all sitting with their backs toward me. One of them rose. It was a woman. She walked to the other side of the fire, but her face was not yet visible to me, since she was peering out over the somber sea. She stood thus for a while, and then turned. It was Mrs. Meredith!

Throwing all of my former caution to the winds, I breasted my way boldly enough through the high sedge, and called out Dr. Meredith's name. The sound of a human voice issuing from the unknown shadows that surrounded them seemed to electrify the little group. For a moment they remained as motionless as if they were frozen. Then the voice of Dr. Meredith answered: "Who is there?"

In a moment more I was among them. I was received like one returned from the dead. Mrs. Meredith cried and kissed me, Dr. Meredith shook my hand warmly, and Grame administered a huge thump on my back.

"We feared you were dead," said Dr. Grame.

"Well, I'm not," I returned; "so tell me how you happened to be here."

It is impossible to record the ensuing conversation. Naturally every one talked at once, and we heard each other's stories in fragments. When I asked where Eleanor and Nicky were, Mrs. Meredith burst into tears. I had decided not to speak of my finding Eleanor—it would have done no good, and would have only upset them. It was better to let them think that their daughter was tossing around in the sea on a bit of wreckage, or even that she was drowned, rather than to inform them that she was in the power of some unknown person or thing somewhere in the darkness that lay all around us.

So I told my story, leaving out Eleanor's part in it, and heard their story, bit by bit. I had learned of the first part through Eleanor, so I will take it up from the time of the wreck. The Merediths, Dr. Grame and the sailor, George, were in one boat. The captain was to have been in this boat, but George and Grame had seized the oars and pulled after Eleanor. The search for the girl was fruitless, but Don Endon, the young underengineer who had plunged in after Eleanor, was picked up.

The captain and the crew manned the other lifeboat; the two tiny craft were soon separated by the violence of the storm. The night had been very miserable, with the splashing of the cold spray, and the tireless tossing of the boat. No one slept. When morning came they saw the shore of Large Island near, and landed. They had food and water in the boat, and were quite comfortable after they had dried out before a smoking fire of wet wood.

Nicky had disappeared in the forenoon, and their chief occupation since had been in searching for him. There was no
trace of his departure, so it was only a matter of conjecture
where he had gone or what had happened to him.

While the Merediths told their story I was supplied with an
extra pair of shoes that fitted me poorly, and was given some
roast fish and half a can of beans. The ship-wrecked party had
quite a supply of food and water, for the captain had been very
careful to see that the boat was loaded with as many stores as
it could safely carry. Consequently the men had made no effort
to find any native food, except to catch a few fish in various
ways.

Dr. Grame had improvised a net from his shirt and a branch,
and could bag as many small fish as he wished in a short time.
As Dr. Meredith had said, most of the time had been spent in
searching for Nicky.

As was to be expected, Mrs. Meredith was terribly broken
up over the loss of her two children. She had cried until there
were no more tears in her to shed, and was now living in a sort
of coma. It was evident that her health was in a precarious state.
Dr. Grame told me on the side that he would not be surprised
at a nervous breakdown. The conversation dragged on for about
half an hour, while I learned all the details of their experience.

The moon had risen and was lighting up the landscape
brightly. Its long, streaked reflection on the quivering water was
forlornly beautiful. I had learned all the news, and the talk had
drifted into theories of the fate of the young Merediths, the
chance of our being rescued soon, and how long the water
supply would last. My mind returned repeatedly to the smoke
I had seen on Crescent Island. I would certainly go there that
very night, but should I take any one with me? And how could
I get away from the rest of the party?

While thinking over these matters I strolled to the beach to
have a look at the lifeboat. It was a light, strongly built dory.
Fortunately the supplies had been transferred from it to a tar-

paulin shelter on the shore. I would have to go in the boat. How else could I bring Eleanor back in case I should find her?

Then another thought entered my mind. Suppose I should be killed, or should lose the boat in some way or other? Was it fair to the little party huddled around the camp fire to expose them to the risk of being deprived of their boat? But then I had to take the boat if I wished to save Eleanor; and that settled the question for me.

Finding that there were no oars in sight, I peered into the boat. There were none there. This was very annoying. I would either have to find the oars or ask where they were. This would demand some sort of an explanation. Hence it was not unnatural that I should mutter an oath.

"And why curse, pray?" asked a voice nearby.

Turning about sharply, I saw Dr. Grame standing beside me, his hand resting on the butt of a pistol in the holster at his side.

"Oh, you there," I said, trying to be nonchalant. "Didn't hear you come up. What do you think of this mess?"

"I think we all know things the other fellow doesn't. Wouldn't it be better to come out with them and all pull together?"

"What do you mean?" I demanded, feigning to miss his meaning. "What do I know that you do not?"

Grame regarded me narrowly for a moment, and then said:

"Well, in the first place, you know something about Eleanor— and for my part I know some rather interesting things about Nicky. We both have reasons, perhaps, for not telling the Merediths, especially at this time. But if we compared notes, many things might be cleared up. Come now, am I not right?"

"You are, undoubtedly," I answered, "and I shall do as you wish. But first, how did you know I had any knowledge of Eleanor?"

He smiled and took a step toward me.

"By that," he said, tapping the gun that hung at my side. "It's good I know you, or I would have suspected underhand work."

Eleanor's revolver! What a fool I had been! No wonder Grame suspected that I knew something about Eleanor.

"You recognized it?" I asked. "Do you suppose any of the others did?"

"No," he replied. "It's my own gun— that's why I recognized it. I gave it to Eleanor when we first struck the reef."

"Good," I muttered. "Now sit down, and I will tell you all about it."

I had no idea what a relief talking would be. However, when I came to my carelessness that night on Devil's Island, I broke down and cursed myself roundly. Grame clapped me on the back, almost driving it through my chest, and commanded me to pull myself together. He assured me that I was not to blame; that the catastrophe would have occurred if I had kept awake.

When I spoke of the smoke on Crescent Island, he cursed and said:

"We'll go there this very night. You and I will start immediately."

He made as if to rise, but I caught his belt and dragged him down again.

"Wait a minute," I commanded him. "There's just one thing more."

Then I told him about the dead monkey I had seen, and reminded him of the skeleton on Devil's Island. They were huge, powerful beasts, and probably vicious. Whether they would actually attack a person, I did not know.

When I had finished talking, Grame sat in silence. Then he spoke.

"I don't understand the presence of such creatures in the West Indies," he said. "This is something new to me. I don't see how they could have existed here without having been discovered before. The only explanation I can offer is that they have been carried here on a floating island, from Africa, which might have drifted north with some current. But at all events, they *are* here; so it is not our task at present to explain their presence, but to discover whether they are dangerous. Well, let's be on our way to Crescent Island."

I suggested that if we were going away we ought to warn Charley and the engineer. They could be on the lookout and protect the Merediths.

"You are right, Jimmy," he said. "I'll get them down here on the pretense of helping launch the boat. I'll tell the people that you and I are going to row down the shore and have a final look for Nicky before we turn in. Incidentally, I'll tell you some interesting facts about the young gentleman on the way."

Grame stalked back to the camp fire. I could hear him talking to the Merediths. In a few minutes he was back with Charley and Don at his heels. He invited them to sit down, and explained the danger of the apes to them.

"Now, men," he said, "Jimmy and I are going down the shore in the boat. Here is my gun and a belt of cartridges. Don't use it unless you have to; ammunition is scarce hereabouts. If we don't come back by morning, don't expect us back. We'll be where we can't come back. Don't let Mrs. Meredith hear about any of this. She is very nervous, and the shock might cause a collapse."

Turning to me, he said: "All right, Jimmy, let's go."

With the aid of the two men we launched the dory, and climbed in.

"You might bring us the oars from behind that palm tree to your left," called Dr. Grame to Charley.

The man found them in a trice, and we began our journey, each at an oar.

"How do we get to this island?" asked Dr. Grame.

"We go to the left of the little island we are headed for. Ours is the next one after it. You can spot it right away by its crescent shaped beach."

"Well, we're off," murmured the doctor. "The sooner we arrive, the better. Guess we had better take it easy now; we may need our strength on the return trip."

We rowed at a leisurely rate, our oars splashing softly, the only sound in the night. There was no wind, and the moon was climbing up the eastern sky. The surface of the ocean was rolling gently, and tossed the reflection of the moon in long, swinging arcs.

I had rowed at night before, but never with such emotions stirring in my heart. I was looking for the girl I loved, seeking to rescue her from the power of the unknown. My aid in this task was an eccentric and impetuous scientist. However, I was glad that it was Dr. Grame who was with me. I felt that he was a man to be relied on.

We rowed in silence for some time. At last Grame spoke.

"Jimmy," he said, "I am going to tell you what I think of this whole affair. It may strike you as absurd—as the fantasy of a mind steeped in science. Nevertheless, I'm sure I'm right—at last. Do you know who threw you overboard?"

"No," I answered, "do you?"

"I can guess," was his reply. "Unless I am greatly mistaken, Nicky gave you the crack on the head, and then helped you over the rail."

I was not surprised. In fact, I agreed with him, and told him so.

"But on what do you base your conclusion?" I asked.

"Well, it's this," answered Grame. "Everyone suspects that Nicky is a bit odd. He is odd—damn odd. Do you know anything about biology?"

I had to admit that I knew little.

"Well, I'll give you a lesson on this interesting subject before I go on with Nicky's case. You have probably heard that man is descended from the ape. That is not quite true. He is the brother of the ape; they both had the same forefathers, so to speak. But the origin of man lies even farther back than the parent of the monkey.

"Monkeys, dogs, horses, ourselves and countless other animals originated from a creature that in turn is descended from the amphibian. The latter developed from an even lower form of life, which came itself from one-celled animals—so small that they are visible only under the microscope. This sounds imaginative, fantastic. Nevertheless it is accepted by scientists, and many laymen. Eventually it will be admitted by everyone.

"This is a fact that has been believed since the time of Darwin—since before him, in fact. However, we now have to take up a newer idea. Many biologists hold that the individual, in its development, retraces the development of the human race. Every creature begins life in the form of a one-celled organism, so small as to be invisible except to the microscope.

"That is the way the human race began life. As the egg develops, the embryo has gill slits—just as the human race went through the fish period, and breathed through gills. Man still has a small vermiform appendix, an organ that is found in the body of the rabbit, whose function is the digestion of grass. In the rabbit, it is large. It was also large in man while mankind was going through the grass eating stage; but since man has given up this food, the appendix has shrunk in size, and remains only as a vestige of the past. In time it will probably entirely disappear.

"I will not go into details. These are a few illustrations to enable you to understand what I say. So you see that each individual, in his development, recapitulates the development of the human race. In the world of science this is called the Biogenetic Law, or the Law of Recapitulation.

"This recapitulation is physical, as stated in the law. However, it is my opinion that one's soul, one's intellect—one's physiological and psychological makeup—go through the same process of recapitulation. Now I believe that Nicky, in his development, has carried into life a strain of the primeval; a tinge of the beast. He is wavering between two possibilities—it is a matter of chance whether he will become perfectly normal in a very short time, or whether he will become a beast in his nature. At present he is a combination. At one time he is a perfect little angel; as nice a child as you could want. At other times he is a devil, and behaves as if he were a wild animal. Even his physical appearance changes.

"During the time you have known him, he has been quite normal. But the morning after your disappearance I noticed a change in him. I strongly suspected that he had been a wild animal that night, and had reverted back to himself with the day.

"I have never seen him when he was having one of these spells—I have only seen him on the edge of them, or just after he has recovered. They leave their mark. I don't know whether he is intelligent when he becomes a beast, or whether he is as other beasts are. I know that his body does not change, except in minor ways.

"His family think they have seen him in these periods, but they haven't. They, as I, have only seen him on the boundary line. He is in a much worse condition than they imagine. I haven't told them, because it would only have caused them unnecessary worry if he should turn out all right. If he doesn't— well, there is nothing that can be done for him, so why upset the poor people any more than they are already?"

I agreed with Dr. Grame on this point. However, his recital seemed very strange. Yet I could not help believing him. The way he put it was so plausible. I asked many questions, but was convinced from the first.

During the course of Dr. Grame's talk we had drawn very near the white sand beach of Crescent Island. We ceased talking, and rowed silently. Then I could feel the bottom of the boat grating on the sand.

"Better give me your knife," whispered Grame as we dragged the boat up on the beach, and made it fast to a large log half submerged in the sand.

I offered him the gun, but he refused, saying that he could get along with a knife.

"Where was the smoke?" he asked.

"I think I know the general direction," I answered, and we set out along the shore, hugging the edge of the woods, and walking quietly.

CHAPTER VIII

A SCREAM IN THE DARK

THE TIDE WAS almost at the flood, and we were forced to plod along in the loose sand that is never packed down by the water. This made walking difficult, and materially retarded our progress.

We advanced for some time in silence. Then Grame spoke,

"What are the chances of our locating the source of that smoke?"

"I found your fire without much trouble," I answered, "but luck was with me."

Grame grunted.

"Do you see the palm trees ahead of us?" I asked, "I'll climb one of those, and have a look around."

The trees were about a quarter of a mile away, on a small promontory. If a fire were burning anywhere on the island, it should have been visible from one of the palms.

Our advance was suddenly checked by a loud splash.

"What was that?" I demanded.

"Look out there!" he replied, pointing his finger.

For a moment I saw nothing but water and sky. Then a dark form broke up through the water, hovered in the air, and fell back with a resounding splash.

"What in Heaven's name!" gasped Grame.

"Looked like a whipray," I answered. "They have that little trick."

"Oh, I know the whipray. Has wings-swims as a bird flies. Long tail with a bunch of barbed arrows that it can sling into you."

"That's it," I answered.

By the time we had finished discussing the peculiarities of the whipray, we had arrived at the palm grove. I chose the tallest and undertook the ascent. Climbing a palm is no easy task. The trunk is smooth and slippery, and all its branches are in a cluster at the very top of the tree.

Several trials were necessary before I finally managed to reach the fans. I drew myself up into a sitting position, and looked about. But my efforts were wasted. Far and near, there was no trace of a fire, or anything that would denote the presence of humans or monkeys. I remained aloft for several minutes, straining my eyes, but to no avail. However, I did get an idea of the geography of the island. Its shore line formed a triangle, whose base was the crescent shaped beach. Thus we were on one of the vertices.

I descended and informed Grame of the failure of my observations.

"Well, you can't expect success in the first attempt," was his philosophic comment.

After some consideration, we decided to continue on down the shore line, and strike inland later on. It was going to be a difficult matter to find the fire, or the place where the fire had been. Here we were, on an island several square miles large, trying to find a spot the size of a door mat. If we did run across it, it would be by the merest luck. But chance had been friendly to me from the very first of the voyage, so I did not despair.

The stars above us were very bright, and the sky was illumined by the full moon. As I watched the twinkling spots, I wondered if on their surface any searches such as ours were taking place. Was any man on that very bright one looking for the girl he loved? We were small and insignificant, after all. Why should providence bother with such mites as Dr. Grame and myself?

Grame interrupted my star-gazing by a low exclamation.

"Footprints!"

"Where?" I asked.

"Not in the sky, at any rate," he answered with a little laugh. "Right ahead of you. See 'em?"

Grame was not mistaken. High up on the beach, out of the reach of the waves, were a group of indistinct prints. Half obliterated by the wind and spray, they were still recognizable. A couple of the more perfect ones seemed to have been made by a big flat foot with extremely long toes. The others were merely depressions, partly filled by the blowing sand.

"This bunch must have landed here," at length remarked my companion.

"Do you see any mark of a boat in the sand?" I asked.

"No. They probably landed at low tide. The prints seem to lead up from the water."

I suggested that we look around a bit for the boat or raft; I thought that it might have been carried into the sedge grass bordering the shore. We searched for several minutes, but found nothing.

"What kind of prints are they?" I asked.

"Impossible to say exactly," he answered, "however, it looks to me as if they had been made by some of your monkey friends. What do you think?"

I did not answer him; I was wondering whether it could have been the apes who had abducted Eleanor. It was not a pleasant thought.

"Have you seen any marks that could have been made by a shoe?" I asked.

"I thought of that, too, son," Grame answered. "I've looked carefully, but all of the prints seem to be of the same kind. I can't say yet whether Eleanor was in this band or not."

"How many do you think landed here?" I demanded.

"Hard to tell. I should say about seven or eight, but I may

be way off. It's perfectly possible that any number more might have remained nearer the water; in that case their prints would have been washed away by the waves."

The marks in the sand led down the beach. After we had taken another good look about, we set out to follow them. Here at last was a clue, and trailing it was more liable to bring results than beating the island blindly.

"You had better keep your gun at hand; no telling when something might turn up," Grame warned me.

We watched the prints closely, hoping to find one made by a shoe. We saw several that Eleanor might have made, but these were so filled with loose sand that it was really impossible to make sure. There was always the possibility that Eleanor had walked further down on the firm sand, in which case the marks made by her shoes had been eradicated by the water.

At length we came to a place where the markings disappeared. After a close examination, it seemed quite evident that the party had turned inland. We were able to track them for a while by the trampled grass and torn creepers, but at length these tell-tale signs were left behind.

"All we can do now is to trust to luck, and cruise around at hazard," said Grame. "You might try crawling up a tree again."

This time I found a live oak, taller and easier to climb than a palm. The view from the topmost branches was beautiful, but disappointing. I could see no traces of living beings. Below me was a dense mass of trees, vines, and bushes, shining in the pale light of the moon. Beyond the dark shadow of the land, the ocean lay bright and calm. The only sounds were the rustling of the leaves in a light breeze, the creaking of branches, and an occasional croak from a bird awakened.

I slid down and joined Grame.

"What luck?" he asked.

"None at all."

We started out again, walking in long zigzags, as a ship tacks against the wind. In this way we were able to cover a great deal of ground.

After half an hour spent in beating the woods in this manner, we stopped to rest a moment. It was hot work forcing a way through the tangle of foliage; the briers tore our clothing; and the smaller creepers had an annoying way of twining about our legs and tripping us.

"My word," grunted Grame, "this is a regular jungle. We'll be at this all night before—"

His words were cut short by a scream— loud, hoarse, awful, enough to strike fear into the heart of any man. Grame seized my arm; we listened breathlessly. The scream was not repeated, but it seemed to vibrate through the whole island. Several dismal croaks came back from the roosting birds.

"Death in the grave!" gasped my companion. "What a noise, what a noise!"

I shivered.

"What do you suppose *that* was?" asked the doctor when he had recovered his composure.

"Couldn't say," I replied. "It sounded like almost anything horrible."

"Hope it doesn't come our way, that's all."

Then I thought of Eleanor. She might have been within two feet of the thing that had filled Grame and me with horror and dread.

"Come on," I said, "we've got to go in the direction of that sound."

"Right. I wonder whether monkeys can scream like that?"

The cry had come from our right. We made our way in that direction, moving cautiously.

"It couldn't have been very far away," said Grame. "Keep your eyes open."

I went first with the gun, and Grame followed with the knife. The shadows ahead were dense; we could see nothing in them.

My ankle turned, and I sank on my knees with a muttered curse. Looking to see what I had stepped on, a familiar object lay before my eyes; an object that filled me with excitement and hope.

"Look at this," I whispered.

"A shoe," gasped Grame. "A woman's shoe!"

"Eleanor's," I said. "I remember it."

"Then she came this way. It's probable she isn't far from us now. Go on."

We started off.

"Better crawl," grunted my companion. "Believe I heard something ahead."

He was right. I rather felt than heard it. It was one of those vibrant, pulsing noises.

"No crawling for mine," I whispered in his ear. "I prefer to keep on my feet. I'd advise you to do the same."

The sound continued. After we had advanced a short distance it was apparent that a clearing was in front of us. Streaks of moonlight were visible, and the woods were lighter. A moment later my guess was confirmed. We stood on the edge of a small clearing. In it lay numerous objects, lit up by the moon. Grame drew up beside me, and we stood gazing, not daring to breathe.

CHAPTER IX

THE MISSING BOAT

HOW LONG I would have stood thus I do not know. Grame had more presence of mind, and drew me behind a large live oak. We looked at each other in silence.

"Did you see her?" asked Grame.

"No," I replied, did you?"

"No."

"Well, we've got to find out whether she is there, and which one she is," I whispered, almost to myself.

The noise I spoke of before still persisted. I gradually realized what it was—the sobbing of a woman. I whispered my conviction to Grame, and he agreed.

"She is evidently there, and awake. We must attract her attention, without awakening the rest. We've got to sneak her away if possible; they're too many for gun play. How many cartridges have you?"

"About twenty," I answered.

"Well, you'd get about ten apes, and then they would get us all. Save your gun for use if they wake up. How can we attract Eleanor's attention without arousing the suspicions of the rest?"

I thought quickly.

"We might try whistling a tune. If the apes did hear it the chances are they would think it was a bird."

"All right, try it," whispered Grame.

I began to whistle "Good Night, Ladies." Why I picked this

particular tune is more than I can say. It was a weird scene. There we were in the very lair of a band of savage apes, and one of us was whistling "Good Night, Ladies!" It is far from a cheerful melody at best; under these circumstances it was positively eerie. I shall never hear the tune again without a shudder.

But its smooth air had effect. The sobbing ceased. My glance roved from one prostrate form to another in an effort to locate Eleanor as soon as possible. She had evidently heard the tune, but did not realize the full significance of it. It would dawn on her, I thought.

And then one of the bodies rose slowly and began to look around. I stepped out into the moonlight and continued to whistle softly. Another body moved slightly and grunted. I quit whistling. The body that had raised itself peered at me intently for a moment, and then waved. It was Eleanor.

My joy was so great that I thought the pounding of my heart would surely awaken the apes. I prayed that Eleanor would not make any noise. Slowly, ever so slowly, she crept toward us through the sleeping forms. I followed her course with the muzzle of my revolver, ready to send a bullet through the first ape that hindered her advance. It seemed centuries before she reached us.

"Thank God!" were her first words.

"Here's your shoe," was my abrupt reply, as I gave her the frail pump I had unconsciously held in my hand.

"Come!" whispered Grame. "There's no time to lose."

Eleanor detained him with a gesture.

"Nicky's there!" she whispered. "He has gone mad. I can't leave him."

"I'll go wake him," I volunteered.

"No! No!" said Eleanor hastily. "He would give us away. He has attached himself to those things. If he wakes he will surely cry out."

"We'll both go," said Grame, drawing out a handkerchief.

"We'll gag him with this. If he tries to gurgle I'll cut off his wind. We will carry him with us."

I must admit that the thought of exposing Eleanor to danger again almost made me object to this plan, yet I knew she would never forgive me if I did. So I asked:

"Which one is he?"

Eleanor pointed out her brother to us and we began to crawl toward the sleeping band. As we left, Grame whispered to the girl.

"If there's any trouble stay behind the tree."

It was delicate work. We passed the first sleeper without mishap, Grame in the lead. As we approached the second ape, he groaned and flapped his arms. We crouched down, hardly breathing. However, he gave no more signs of awakening, and we continued our advance. Two were passed in safety; nevertheless I could not help thinking of our return trip with Nicky. Would we be able to keep him quiet? It was a big chance. Then we reached him.

He was lying on his left side with his face away from us, apparently asleep. I crawled up beside Grame, who motioned to me that I was to seize Nicky when he gave the word. He seemed to hesitate before applying the gag. Who wouldn't have hesitated? How large a chance did we have of extracting a sleeping boy from the midst of thirty or more sleeping apes, especially when the boy did not wish to be carried away? The wind sighed through the leaves of the forest, and some crawling thing rustled over the dried twigs nearby.

"**WISH** I had some chloroform," breathed Grame. "Pick him up and carry him. Put one arm under his shoulders and one under his knees. He won't make any noise until several seconds after he has awakened. By that time I will have him so he can't squeal."

According to instructions I lifted Nicky in my arms, and started toward Eleanor, with Grame at my side. He was watching Nicky's face intently. The sleeping boy showed no signs of waking.

Several of the apes stirred as we slowly made our way to the edge of the clearing. However, we did not let this stop us—we were too near freedom.

Finally we reached Eleanor. We struck out for the beach, walking noiselessly. Our progress was slow indeed. I could not see where I was putting my feet, and Grame had his eyes glued on Nicky's face. It fell to Eleanor to lead the way, while I kept her in the general direction of the shore.

Each moment carried us further from the apes, and gave us a little more hope. Quite naturally we increased our speed. Nicky turned out to be a much sounder sleeper than I had dared hope.

Grame took him when I was almost tired out, and I watched for his awakening. However, this did not come. As I continually looked at his face I could not help noticing what a change had come into it.

Nicky was no longer the little boy who had built card houses on the Mermaid. His face was the face of a cunning, sly criminal. His upper teeth protruded slightly over his lower lip, and the skin at the corners of his mouth had become taut. It was surprising that a person with such a face could sleep so soundly. I mentioned this to Grame. He nodded his head and said:

"Once again we find him, but on the border line—otherwise he would not be asleep now. When he wakes he will perhaps be almost normal. No one can say."

The underbrush became less dense; soon we were back at the beach again.

"We'll have to wake him now," said the doctor. "We had better run while we can. He can do that more efficiently if he is awake."

Grame laid him on the sand and shook him violently. His eyes opened and he glanced around blankly for a moment. Then his gaze fell on us. An ugly snarl spread over his face and his mouth started to open. Quick as a flash Grame closed his fingers over Nicky's throat and thrust the handkerchief in his mouth.

A gurgle was all that resulted from the child's attempt to scream. Grame adjusted the handkerchief, and with the aid of a small stick made a perfect gag. Nicky could not make a sound louder than a whisper.

"Now, young man," began Grame, "you're going to come with us, and you're not going to make any noise, or try to get away—understand? If you do I'll tan the hide off you."

Nicky only made a snarling noise and lifted his hand to the gag. Grame gave him four resounding slaps in the face that brought a little cry from Eleanor. But if these blows pained Eleanor, they pained Nicky also, for he rose quickly to his feet, and let his hands remain at his sides.

"Still on the border," muttered Grame to me as he took off his necktie and bound Nicky's hands behind his back. When he had tied the last knot, he turned to me and said:

"You help Eleanor, and I'll give Nicky a hand. We've got to run. They may be after us any minute now."

I took Eleanor's arm, Grame seized the shoulder of Nicky's shirt, and we were off. Eleanor was game, and so was Nicky.

He knew he had to do as he was told, and it was wonderful the way he held out. In a very short time we were at the grove of palm trees. We walked for a while here, to give Eleanor and Nicky a chance to get their breath. I was glad to rest myself. As for Grame, I don't believe he was at all tired.

The doctor did not let us tarry long. He gave the word and we set out again at a fast trot. The distance was shorter than I had thought it. We passed several odd shaped stumps that I remembered. The boat should have been quite near now. However, it was not in sight. There was a curve in the coast line several hundred yards away—had we left the boat just around the bend?

"Where in the name of science is that boat?" said Grame, coming to a halt.

"It must be around the bend up there," I answered.

"We left it on this side," asserted the doctor.

"Are you sure?"

"Quite."

We stood and looked at each other.

"Well, let's go on anyway; perhaps we did leave it there," Grame conceded.

We took up the trot again, but I soon saw an object that caused me to stop short. It was the log we had tied the boat to. I recognized it, and also the two little mangroves nearby.

"It's gone," I said briefly. Grame ran down to the cape while Eleanor and I looked in the grass and along the edge of the woods. We found nothing, not even footprints. Grame returned and reported that he had seen no signs of our boat.

"Well, it's gone. What are we going to do?" I asked.

"Swim, I guess," was his verdict.

"S-h! Listen," Eleanor broke in.

We held our breath and did as commanded. From the hammock came a crackling noise from the tangle. It sounded like a party of people or things pursuing us.

"Swim?" asked Grame.

Eleanor and I assented.

"I'll take the child," said the doctor. "You and Eleanor look after, each other."

"We will only have to go as far as the first island," I said. "The raft is there."

"Good enough," answered Grame. "Let's get started."

The swim to Little Island was tiring, but apparently we were not seen. Grame left the gag in Nicky's mouth, and we arrived among the mangroves undiscovered. A short walk brought us to the cove where I had left the raft. It was still there, fast among the roots of the surrounding trees. We disentangled It, pulled off a couple of planks for paddles, and after half an hour's labor, arrived safely at the Merediths' camp.

Grame removed the gag from Nicky's mouth, and we pulled the raft high and dry on shore, aided by George and Don, who had remained awake and heard our approach.

CHAPTER X

ELEANOR'S STORY

KISSING, TEARS, LAUGHTER and bustling about followed. Nothing would satisfy Mrs. Meredith but that she feed her heaven-returned children with her own hand. It was a gay little party that was gathered around the roaring camp fire; gay in spite of the grim situation in which it found itself.

Nicky was treated as if he were the soul of virtue. Dr. Grame had warned Mrs. Meredith that her son had been temporarily out of his head, probably because of fright and privation. He added that it would be better not to ask him any questions concerning his disappearance and subsequent adventures; it would merely upset him, and perhaps derange his mind.

We had all lived up to the doctor's instructions, and no curiosity had been shown about his or Eleanor's adventure. We all sat around the fire, and were just glad to see each other again, until Nicky's head began to nod, and finally lay against his mother's shoulder. "You had better put him to bed," said Grame, indicating the tarpaulin shelter. "He's sound asleep. I would suggest that you do not leave his side, Strange things have been going on in him up here," he added, tapping his head.

I lifted Nicky and carried him to the tarpaulin. There was a large pile of palm leaves and sedge grass hard by, gathered by George. We constructed two beds, and put Nicky on one.

Before I returned to the fire, Mrs. Meredith made me tell her of the rescue. I did so, briefly enough, asking her forgiveness for not having told her of Eleanor when I had first found the party. Of course she forgave me and added:

"I want to hear the details so much. But as Dr. Grame says, my place is here. I owe a double debt to you both—may God bless two of the bravest men in the world!"

With that she kissed me on the cheek.

When I returned to the group around the fire, Dr. Grame was in the midst of explaining Nicky's situation. As I sat down by Eleanor, the doctor turned to me and said:

"I was just telling them. We are probably in for more trouble with the apes. It is necessary that we all understand Nicky. It may save lives."

I agreed with him, and he continued his explanation. I had heard it once, and it did not hold my attention now. I could not help watching the faces of the listeners as Dr. Grame unfolded his remarkable theory. George listened with a half incredulous, half puzzled expression. Don paid careful attention, and it was evident that the subject was not new to him. Dr. Meredith drank in every word eagerly, but it was not hard to see that he was suffering.

He had probably known for a long time that Nicky was not normal. He was glad to hear this explanation; anything was better than uncertainty. As for Eleanor, she comprehended but vaguely, and could not repress an occasional sob, although during the flight from Crescent Island she had been as brave as any of us. Who could blame the poor girl for crying now? When I thought of what she had been through I shuddered.

At length Grame concluded, and Dr. Meredith asked:

"Do you think he remembers what he has done since he left us?"

"There is no doubt about it. He does. In his good moments he remembers perfectly well his actions in his bad moments. I'm glad you brought this point up. As long as he does remember these bad periods, you may know he has turned neither way.

"If ever the time comes when he does not remember these

times, you may be certain that his development has come through the critical period, and that he will always be quite normal. In his bad moments he remembers who he is—that he is a human. Should he ever forget this he is gone forever."

"What can be done for him?" the father almost begged.

"Nothing here," answered Grame softly, "nothing but kind treatment. The more association he has with all of us the better. A shock might cure him, or on the other hand, it might ruin him. If we can get him to New York I know of an apparatus that might— But there, just remember to be kind to him, and see as much of him as possible.

"This is not the sort of case that is helped by punishment of any sort. Whatsoever he does is through no desire of his own. He cannot keep from doing it; that is all." After Grame had concluded his discussion of Nicky's condition, all were eager to hear Eleanor's story. The reader already knows part of it, so we will take up her narrative at the point where she fell asleep on Devil's Island.

"I awoke suddenly. Some one was holding my arms tightly behind my back while they were being tied. I cried out, again and again.

"When my hands were tied I was dragged to my feet. At first I could see nothing. The moon had set; everything was dark. I was horribly frightened. But when I saw those apes standing around me in a circle, all grinning—"

The poor girl stopped. The memory was too much for her. However, she continued after a moment:

"I saw Jimmy lying on the ground. An ape, very much smaller than the rest, rolled him over, and then gave him a kick. As the ape turned, the light fell on its face. It was Nicky! At first I thought he was a captive, too—but only for a moment. A second look at his face told me he was mad.

"I called to him; I pleaded with him, but he would not listen. Two apes seized me by the arms and dragged me along between them. I stumbled frequently, but they held me up. We reached the shore and got into three long, narrow boats.

"Nicky was in the boat with me. He would not talk to me, would not listen to me. At length I gave up trying to reason with him.

"He seemed to be in command of our boat. He jabbered to the apes who were paddling with boards or flattened limbs, and seemed to have trouble in making himself understood.

"We reached the island you found me on while it was still dark. Nicky ordered me to get out, and the whole party landed, except a few who stayed in the canoes, and paddled them up the shore.

"We walked inland until we came to a large clearing—not the one you found us in to-night. There were a lot of hut things there; made of branches and leaves. We met more monkeys here. There were about fifty altogether.

"They put me in one of the huts, with guards on the outside. The thing smelled awfully. At last the sun came up; I could see it through the openings in the wall.

"I don't know what had been happening outside; but suddenly there was an uproar. The apes were all jabbering and screaming. Those things are almost human. I've seen monkeys before, but none like those. I suppose they are the missing links; anyway, they are just like people in many ways.

"The jabbering kept up. Then I heard a noise outside of my hut, and Nicky came in with an ugly old ape. The thing really bowed to me—then stood and looked at me, all over."

I thought she was going to have to stop again—but she only shuddered, and kept on bravely enough.

"They jabbered at each other for a minute or two. Then the thing bowed to me again, and went out with Nicky. A minute later Nicky came back in, and untied my hands and told me to follow him.

"When I came out of the hut every ape in the clearing was looking at me. The one who had come in with Nicky stepped up to my side. I really recognized him. They are just like people that way. No two look alike. I can't tell one Chinaman from another, but I could those apes.

"The silence lasted several minutes. They all just stood and looked. You can't imagine how awful it was. At last one huge ape that stood in front of the others began to jabber. He turned toward the rest and made motions with his arms. He pointed at Nicky, who stood looking like a young devil.

"When the ape finished talking, the others stood still, looking from one to another. I hadn't the slightest idea what was taking place. They looked from the orator to the ape beside me, and then at Nicky.

"It was evident that the situation, whatever it might be, was strained. Then the ape beside me began to advance on the orator slowly. The others stood back. The one who had jabbered crouched and awaited the attack. I knew instinctively that they were going to fight. Oh, it was fearful! They fought for at least an hour. I have never heard such awful screams. They fought on the ground, in the trees and in the air; the others just standing still and looking.

"They fought locked in close embrace—strangling, biting, clawing. For a long time neither had an apparent advantage. Then the one who had come into my hut bore his adversary to the ground, and sank his teeth in the other's throat. The massive jaws held like a vise, and after much struggling and sobbing, the talker died.

"The victor was borne away almost exhausted, and Nicky seemed to take command of the rest of the band. I tried to question him, but he ordered me to return to the hut. I did so immediately; I had no desire to be dragged there by a couple of apes.

"About an hour later Nicky came in with a gourd of coconut milk, some cooked fish, and coconut meat. I was hungry enough and ate heartily. While I ate my meal, Nicky sat and eyed me with a thoughtful expression. When I had finished he asked me if I had noticed the ape who had accompanied him into the tent earlier and who had been the victor in the death struggle.

" 'He is the chief of this band now,' Nicky told me. 'The one he killed used to be. I am to be the leader of all the tribes. The former ruler of this one opposed me, and you know what happened to him!'

"I saw it was no use to try to dissuade him or bring him to his senses. He was no longer a child. Yet I made the attempt and tried to get him to sit in my lap. However, it was to no avail. So I said to him:

" 'Why did you take me outside to see the fight? You knew I did not want to!'

" 'I took you out to see whether the people would stand beside Uglub (he called those hairy things—people!). Uglub was second in power. He promised to kill the chief and support me. You are to stay with me and help me rule. I desired to see what the people would think of their new chief's sister."

"There is no need to speak of the effect the announcement had on me. I a member of this band of animals. It is a wonder I did not have hysterics. However, I did my best to keep my head, and by a miracle succeeded.

"I knew appealing to him would do no good, so I said nothing. He left the hut and I sat by myself all the afternoon, watching the shadows of the trees slowly lengthen. I thought of attempting an escape, but rejected the idea when I had considered it logically. If I did get away front the apes, would I be in any better position? I determined to wait and see what turned up. I thought Nicky might come to his senses and then we could escape together.

"When night fell there was a great commotion. Nicky came into the hut, and told me we were going to move. What the reason was I do not know. We went through the woods, and met another party."

"The one whose trail we crossed, no doubt," put in Grame. Eleanor continued:

"My shoe came off and they would not let me stop to pick it up. And then we came to the clearing. Nicky and several of the apes sat and jabbered for a long time, Then they all lay down and went to sleep.

"I could not sleep. I just lay awake for hours—it seemed like centuries. I'm afraid I cried. And then I heard whistling. You know the rest."

"But we don't," said her father, nodding toward George and Don. "I'll tell you," said Eleanor. When she finished her tale the gathering around the fire broke up. We were all tired and needed sleep. It was decided that a watch should be kept till morning, each man taking a two-hour shift. Dr. Meredith volunteered to head the list, as he had had some sleep already.

In arranging the beds, I found myself beside Dr. Grame.

"What will be our program for to-morrow?" I asked.

"I should think the best thing would be to make the raft large enough to hold us all," he answered. "If the apes take it into their heads to attack us, we can board the raft and put to sea. If they attack us in their boats, we can shoot them one at a time. I believe we could handle them from the raft with two revolvers."

"Hope they don't get after us before we can make the raft," I remarked. "Have we enough water and provisions?"

Grame thought a minute.

"Yes," he said at length, "with what we can collect from the island. Speaking of water, the keg is down by the boat. It ought to be up here where we can have an eye on it."

I took the hint, and volunteered to get it. Eleanor, who had come up and said she would go with me. We walked down to the beach in silence. The warm breeze, the star-strewn sky, the waves lapping on the white sand—what a contrast to the danger we were in! Nature is not without her appeal even in a moment of stress, so we stopped to admire the tropical beauty of the night.

Then Eleanor spoke.

"This is the second time you have saved my life," she said, and would have continued, but I interrupted. When I insisted that I had not saved her life, she merely said:

"Say what you want—but if you hadn't saved me, I should have killed myself the first chance I got."

I could think of nothing to say in answer, and took her hand in silence. She let her hand remain in mine for a moment, and then gave it a little squeeze.

"Come," she said, "this is no time to be romantic. They're waiting for us."

As we walked back to the tarpaulin shelter, I cursed all water kegs because you have to carry them with both hands.

CHAPTER XI

"THE CAVE!"

THE BRANCHES OF the palm trees shone brightly against the light blue of the early morning sky, and the smell of salt and seaweed was in my nostrils. The rustling of the foliage in the light breeze lulled me toward sleep. The sun was an hour in the sky, and sucking up the dew with its slanting rays. I lay a moment enjoying the deliciousness of the half-awake state; then I remembered our position, and sat up.

There were sleeping forms about me. A little way off, feeding the fire, was Don. They had not awakened me to take my turn as sentinel. I arose guiltily, and walked to the fire, wishing Don a good morning.

He told me that Dr. Meredith had kept watch till sunrise. He himself had awakened then, and persuaded the doctor to turn over the post to him, and try to get some rest. The whole party were now asleep, except George, who had set out to catch some fish with Dr. Grame's net.

The latter fact caused me not a little concern. It was foolish for any of us to separate from the rest—especially when unarmed.

"It seems to me it's time to get busy, if we are going to do anything to-day," I said, "let's wake up everybody but Dr. Meredith."

As a result of much shaking, the camp was soon buzzing with life. Mrs. Meredith and Eleanor set about cooking several crawfish we had at hand. The former called to me for my knife to open a can of hominy, several of which were among our stores, but Grame wisely objected.

"We may need that later," he said. "Let's eat what we can get from the island as long as possible. What has become of my fish net?"

We told him George had taken it about twenty minutes ago, and had not returned yet. It was very foolish to try calling to him because of the possibility of betraying our presence to the apes. It was decided that we should eat first, and if he did not return by the time we had finished, Don and I would go after him.

"We can't afford to separate," said Grame. "Besides, we want to get busy on the raft. It must be made larger."

Roasted crawfish and water made a meager breakfast, yet it tasted good enough to us. When we finished George was still absent. It did no good to rail at his foolishness, so Don and I started out to locate him without further discussion. As we left the fire, Grame said:

"Keep an eye out for anything we could use for the raft."

I started toward the shore; however, Don halted me, and explained that George had intended going to a kind of lake that lay at the end of a long inlet, or creek. There were no fish along the beach, and this pool was nearer than the mangrove shore, which was on the other side of the island.

Thus it was that our path led through the woods, if woods they might be called. The combination of trees, bushes and vines would better be termed a jungle. We made our way with difficulty, winding in and out to escape the denser parts. The gnarled, spreading oaks, with streamers of Spanish moss hanging from their branches like the ghost of a beard from a skeleton's chin; the thick vines winding round and round the trunks of unknown trees, like serpents; the dense foliage overhead that shut out the sun, all combined to create in the place an unnatural and clammy atmosphere. It was cool, dismal and dark. We fought on, calling out George's name from time to time in guarded tones. We saw and heard nothing.

After some fifteen minutes we came to the pool. George was not to be seen. We called several times, and received no reply. Don suggested that the sailor might have changed his mind, and gone to some other part of the island for fish. However, we had come so far to this pool, that I was not content to return until we made a thorough search. I voiced my opinion and Don agreed.

We walked around the edge of the water, keeping a careful eye out for footprints or any other sign of the former presence of a human being. Our search proved to be fruitful; about half way around we found a spot that was covered with the prints of shoes. George had evidently stood here some time, changing his footing frequently. It was on the water's edge, and an ideal place to scoop for fish. The singular thing was that a trail of the same prints led off into the jungle again, toward the other shore.

"That isn't the direction to camp," observed Don. "He must not have found any fish, and left for the other side of the island."

Perhaps George had not found fish, but I saw a quantity—snappers, brilliantly green; blue and yellow parrot fish, angel fish; all kinds of fish, some wheeling about indolently, some darting hither and thither, like arrows.

"Whatever reason he left," I answered, "the only thing to do is to follow his trail."

It led up through a swampy lane between thick walls of foliage. As we made our way along this path, something about the footprints struck me as being odd. I observed them carefully before coming to a conclusion.

"Do you see anything queer about those prints?" I asked Don.

He reflected a minute, and answered:

"Why, yes—they are abnormally far apart."

"Right," I continued. "That means he was running. Now, why was he?"

"Looks kind of bad, doesn't it?" said Don.

It did look bad. I thought of ten reasons why George should leave the pool and run up the lane in the forest; none of these reasons was pleasant to think of.

The lane gradually narrowed; then disappeared. We were in the jungle again, though it was less dense here than I had seen it anywhere else on the island. All trace of George was lost. In order to pick it up again Don and I advanced some little distance apart. We continued the search a short time. Then I heard him call to me:

"Hey! Wait a minute! There is something here that—" his voice trailed off into silence. I waited, and became impatient.

"What is it?" I called.

His reply was unintelligible, so I made my way toward him as quickly as possible. As I approached, he called out, "I've found a cave."

When I reached Don I found him standing in front of a rock ledge some ten feet high. In the face of the ledge was a narrow opening. Beyond the opening we could see but a short way. Don eyed me interrogatively.

"Sure," I said. "Let's go in and see what's there."

In we went, Don taking the lead with me close at his heels. The walls of the cave were about fifteen feet apart, and the ceiling barely cleared our heads. When our eyes became accustomed to the dim light, we could see the end of the cave some thirty feet on. We stumbled over the rough ground, away from the entrance.

"That isn't the end," cried Don, as we drew nearer. "It turns off to the right."

It did; a narrow corridor branched out from the cave and led off to the right, but only for ten feet or so. When we turned into the corridor, another blank wall faced us.

"Not much to explore," muttered Don.

"But it will serve its purpose as a cave as far as we are concerned," I answered.

"Meaning what?"

"That we might find this a handy spot if the apes get too neighborly. They are dangerous in large numbers."

We lost very little time in looking about the cave further. I noticed the opening as we went out, and saw that it could be very easily barricaded with a few planks.

We had been away from the rest of the party some time now. They were probably getting worried about us, so we decided to make for the camp at full speed. No doubt George had returned long ago, and was now wondering whether he should set out to rescue us.

We were soon back at the pool, and then came the struggle through the hammock again. It was such slow going that we decided to go straight toward the shore, and then walk up the beach to our camp.

As we approached the shore, the trees and vines became less thick. Walking was easier, and at times it was possible to see fifty feet or more through the forest.

It was in one of these open spaces that something caught my eye which made me seize Don's arm.

"Look!" I whispered.

His only reply was a gasp.

"Do you suppose—" I began. However, it was no time for words, so we ran up to the figure lying on the ground. It was a man—dead.

Don rolled the corpse over on its back, and we saw the face of George. Not his lined, smiling face, but a face contorted and twisted into a mask of pain and fury. We looked a moment in silence. Then Don rolled the body over again.

"Back broken," he said; then with a sob, "damn whoever did this. I didn't know him very well—but he was a real man."

"We all liked him, Don," I answered.

"We ought to bury him," said my companion; "but I don't believe it would be right to the others to stay away from them any longer."

"You are right, Don. We must hurry back to camp as quickly as we can, else they may be like this, too."

The thought gave us wings. We hated to leave the dead man thus, but our duty to the living called us. We reached the coast, and ran up the beach at full speed.

The sand was soft, and it was a long run, but neither of us tired. The awful thought of what might have happened, or might be happening, to those we had left at the fire drove all else from our minds.

We rounded a bend in the beach; camp came into sight. For one terrible moment I saw no human being; then Dr. Grame came into view and one after another all appeared. We learned later they were gathering material for the raft when they heard our approach.

When we arrived all were waiting excitedly to know what had happened. I told them of George's death in as few words as possible.

"Then they are on this island," said Eleanor. "What are we going to do?"

"The cave!" ejaculated Don.

"What cave?" asked Grame.

We hurriedly explained. Dr. Grame and Dr. Meredith agreed that it would be the only safe place if the apes were present in numbers. Mrs. Meredith was on the point of tears, pressing Nicky to her bosom. Eleanor was quite calm and collected.

A rapid fire conversation followed, and we came to the conclusion that it was useless to try the raft, as it was still far too small. Don and I were to scout in the opposite direction from the cave and attempt to determine where the apes were, and how numerous.

And so the engineer and I set out into the jungle again, while those behind us were busy collecting the food and preparing to move to new quarters in the cavern.

CHAPTER XII

AN ATTACK IN FORCE

OUR RECONNOITERING WAS destined to be short-lived. We had not gone two hundred yards from camp before we heard a noise on our right. We crouched and waited. All was quiet. Then a flat, hairy face appeared among the shrubbery several yards away from us. It was joined by a second. With a roar of fury the two beasts dashed toward us.

My revolver spoke; the leading ape staggered, but maintained his advance. Another shot momentarily checked the second ape. As I was about to fire at the first again, a third appeared. He was behind the other two, and I could not get a shot at him.

Subconsciously I realized it would be better to wound two apes than to kill one. But the last one was screened by his fellows, and the first was almost upon us. A bullet full in the face finished him, but the other two were only a yard away, A hastily fired shot caught the last monkey in the neck and knocked him down.

I felt the arms of the remaining ape closing about my body. Two things were in my favor—the ape had received one bullet in the abdomen, and had not pinned my right arm to my side. I raised the revolver quickly, a glimpse of the beast's red jaws passing under my chin; his hot breath on my neck; these were the impressions I had before the gun exploded, and my eyes were blinded by the ape's blood. The embrace relaxed, and my antagonist sank to the ground.

Wiping my face with my sleeve, I saw all three of the apes

lying dead. My first thought was to reload the gun; then we stood on the defensive a moment or so, awaiting further attack. None came.

"Do you suppose there are any more around?" whispered Don.

"Don't know," I answered. "You take the gun, and I'll climb up this tree and have a look."

The tree had numerous branches, and was easy to climb. In a moment I was high enough to command a view of the entire island and surrounding waters. What immediately caught my attention was a fleet of canoes approaching from Crescent Island. I judged there were about ten of them, with four or five apes in each. They would land in the course of ten or fifteen minutes. A careful scrutiny of the island itself brought to light no traces of apes. Climbing quickly down, I told Don what I had seen, and we started back to the camp at a run.

When we arrived we found the party in great excitement. They had heard the shots, and had feared for our safety. We told them of the approach of the apes. There followed a scene of the greatest bustle and commotion. Quickly collecting everything that we considered of value to us, we started to the cave. I carried the water barrel and various cans of vegetables and meat. Dr. Grame had a part of the raft on his massive back. This we intended to use as a barricade for the entrance. All the rest were laden with the provisions and extra clothing that had been put into the lifeboat.

If our progress to the pool had been difficult early that morning it was trebly so now. We were hampered by our loads, and Mrs. Meredith and Eleanor were handicapped by their skirts. We toiled forward slowly, dragging our various burdens through the clinging creepers, and stumbling repeatedly.

I feared that Mrs. Meredith or Eleanor might faint; the circumstances certainly warranted it, if ever circumstances did. But they both showed great bravery, and trailed along beside us doggedly.

When we arrived at the pool a thing occurred that gave us all a fright. We stopped at the entrance of the lane to rest a moment. No sooner had we done so than Nicky made a break, and started off up the cut at full speed. Don and Grame were after him in a moment. Perceiving that he was being followed, Nicky turned off into the woods, and both he and his pursuers were lost to our sight.

I was tempted to join the chase, but realized it would be foolhardy to leave the women unprotected; Dr. Meredith had no gun.

In a few minutes Grame shouted to us that the young runaway had been captured, and before long all three had re-joined us. Having spent all the time we safely could, we picked up our loads and started off up the lane. This time Nicky accompanied Dr. Grame, who held him by one hand. The chances of a second escape were slight.

We had little difficulty in finding the cave again. Our journey from the pool was much quicker because of the nature of the land. We soon struck the cliff, and after following it a little way, we came to the opening in the rocks.

After we had settled down in the cave and arranged the barricade, Don and I took our places in the entrance, awaiting the appearance of the apes. Time passed, but not one of our foes was seen. It was probable that they were having difficulty tracing us.

There was nothing at all to do in our new stronghold, and time hung heavy on every one's hands. Age naturally seeks its own level, and I was not at all surprised when Eleanor joined us behind the barricade.

The conversation jumped from apes to sharks, and from sharks to morays. We spoke of everything. At last food for talk grew very low, and we dealt in personalities. We learned that Don had been three years at Annapolis; had failed to pass some examinations and had been dropped. His presence in Florida and occupation as an underengineer had been the result of his apprehension about his father's temper. Besides he had desired adventure and now his desire was being fulfilled with a vengeance.

Eleanor told us of her school days, and Don and I decided that we were glad that we were not girls.

Our conversation dragged on, and so did the day. At length a brown figure appeared through the woods some hundred yards away. We called to Grame, and had a consultation.

"They'll certainly find us here sooner or later," said the doctor; "might as well let them know right away. Shoot him—it may scare the others off."

I was elected to rid the world of this particular ape. Resting the muzzle of the revolver on a log in the barricade, I took careful aim. The report of the gun was followed by a scream. The simian sank to the ground, out of view among the bushes.

"Number one!" said Don. "Many happy returns of the day."

Our momentary diversion over, we resumed our seats on the hard ground, and tried to think of something cheerful. The sun had passed under a mass of dark clouds, and a chill had come into the air. It looked like rain.

As we sat behind the barricade and talked, it seemed to me that Eleanor was very much interested in Don. It was only natural that she should thank him for diving in the ocean after her the night of the wreck—but was it only natural that she should dwell upon the matter with what struck me as inordinate tenacity? Was she really interested in the fellow? I was unable to answer the question, and my mood grew as dark and taciturn as the weather. I was in my shirt sleeves, and was cold; so I sat hugging myself, and looking gloomily at the woods, taking no part in the conversation.

What would be the end of all this? At the beginning of the voyage, little had I dreamed of a hand-to-hand battle with a shark and withstanding a siege by apes in a dark cave on a West Indian island. After all, there was still some adventure left in the world.

Nicky joined our little group at the mouth of the cave, but I was absorbed in my own thoughts, and paid little attention to him.

Don and Eleanor seemed to be oblivious to my sulky humor, chattering gayly on and addressing a remark to me at intervals. I answered with a grunt. Whether they attributed my curtness to its real cause, or whether they thought I was preoccupied in watching the woods I do not know. At any rate, they left me alone in the end.

I was beginning to weary of the sulks, and wished to join the conversation again, when a low noise caught my ear. I could not tell where it came from. It was barely audible and intermittent. Instead of calling the attention of the others to it I sat still and listened.

It seemed to grow somewhat louder. Of late I had become extremely cautious, so I drew my gun, and held it in readiness. However, the noise died away. I sat with ears alert for at least five minutes, but heard nothing more. Nevertheless, I still kept my gun in hand.

I looked around to call Grame and tell him of the noise, for I had come to rely upon him more than any other of the party. The words were left unsaid, for my eye fell upon Nicky. He was sitting close beside one of the walls, and his face was working queerly. I hardly recognized him. His muscles appeared tense, and his eyes roved restlessly up and down the walls of the cliff—he seemed to be just on the point of doing something.

I have not mentioned it before, but the cliff was bent into the shape of a sharp crescent, and the walls were visible from the opening of the cave for hundreds of yards on either side. If the cliff had been straight, the apes could have crept along the face of the walls, and fallen upon us in large numbers before we were aware of their approach. If they ever managed to tear down our barricade we were lost. They would overwhelm us by sheer numbers.

Following the direction of Nicky's gaze, I half expected to

see a band of apes advancing along the face of the cliff. My fear proved false; there was not a living thing in sight. Evidently the child was about to lapse into the monkey state.

I was on the point of calling Grame when Nicky suddenly leaped up, rushed against the barricade, upset it, and started toward the woods. In an instant I was after him. Just as I was crossing the barricade a hand seized me by the belt, and I was lifted off my feet, and hauled backward. I landed on my back with a thud in time to see Grame pulling our primitive door into place. As he did so a brown body fell from above, hit the barricade as it was rising into position, and landed in front of Eleanor.

The cave rang with the report of two shots from Don's revolver, and the monkey remained still on the floor. By this time the apes were dropping in front of the barricade like brown leaves in autumn. Don and I emptied our revolvers judiciously, decreasing the number of apes as fast as it increased.

We reloaded and emptied several times before the apes gave up the attempt, and broke into headlong flight. We refrained from shooting at them as they fled, for ammunition was too scarce.

When the last of the brown forms had disappeared in the forest, at least twenty lay dead in front of the barricade. The silence that reigned in the cave was broken by convulsive sobs from Mrs. Meredith.

Dr. Grame muttered: "Well, I'll be damned!"

"Good thing Grame nabbed you before you got across the barricade," said Don. "What happened, anyway? First thing I knew we were in the middle of a brown whirlwind."

"Well," said Grame, "I had been hearing a noise from above for some time. I judged from your expression"—turning to me—"that you heard it, too. First thing I knew Nicky was headed for the woods. I realized that the apes were above us on the ledge, ready to jump down and annihilate us. It was a trap to get by the barricade; that noise was monkey talk, I guess.

Evidently Nicky understands it. Thank God I was right behind Jimmy when he started after Nicky."

"I hate to think of the results if you hadn't been," I answered with a shiver.

"Close call," said Don, running a piece of his shirt through the barrel of his revolver. "If they had got by that barricade—well, we wouldn't look like we do now."

Dr. Meredith and Eleanor were at the back of the cave trying to comfort the heartbroken mother. The rest of us remained near the barricade.

So the day passed and the night drew on. No more apes were seen. Grame and I came to the conclusion that they would wait, and try to starve us out. This would not take long, as our provisions would only last us a couple of days more. Our water supply was also getting low. It was perfectly evident that unless the apes wearied of the siege and left us, we would have to devise some means of escape.

We talked the matter over exhaustively, but decided we would attempt nothing that night; we would wait and see what developments the morrow would bring.

Very fortunately the sky had cleared, and the woods were catching the first light from the rising moon. In case of a second attack of the apes, we would at least be able to see. Nevertheless, I felt apprehensive about our safety during the long hours of the night that was to come.

It was decided that a watch of two would be maintained at the barricade throughout the night. Dr. Meredith and I were to take the first turn, from bedtime to one or two in the morning, and Don and Dr. Grame from that time till dawn.

About eight o'clock we all sat down to a very light meal. Don and I sat very near the entrance, needless to say. Mrs. Meredith refused to eat anything, but very bravely joined the group and talked with us while we had our supper.

CHAPTER XIII

A DESPERATE ATTEMPT

A KNIFE DOES not appeal to me, especially when pointed in my direction. So it was with an unpleasant feeling that I watched one slowly creeping down toward my face. What struck me as peculiar was that it was my knife. Now why should my knife be drifting about in the air?

The problem stumped me. As I lay on my back, and watched with half open eyes, the knife descended until it was several inches from my nose and then began to ascend in uneven jumps. As sleep gradually left me, I noticed that the knife was attached to a string, and that the string went through a small hole in the roof of the cave. Without moving my head I could see the backs of Dr. Grame and Don, who were watching the woods.

I was now wide awake, I said to myself, and the knife was a dream. But when I looked above me again the knife was still there, ascending jerkily. Obviously it was being pulled up by some one at the other end of the string.

But who was it, how had he got my knife, and what sense was there in pulling it up and down at the end of a string?

My eyes were glued on the point of the knife. Suddenly it came flying down, right at my face. A quick movement of my head enabled me to let it whiz by my ear into the dirt beside my head. It quivered a moment, and was still. Then the line started to tighten. I seized the knife quickly and snapped the string with a sudden jerk. A muttered exclamation came to my ears in reply.

Whoever was up there had got his aim by letting the knife down on a string, to make sure it would hit me if dropped through the hole. After I was dispatched, the genius above had intended drawing the knife up again. Thus he would have put one of the enemy out of the way without losing a precious weapon.

The knife I held in my hand was my own. Nicky must have taken it from the water keg where I had carelessly left it after opening a can of beans. He had had it concealed on him when he made his escape.

Grame uttered a cry of astonishment when he saw me sitting up with my knife in my hand, examining a string tied to its hilt.

"What in the name of Heaven—" he began. I explained the affair to him.

"Of all the little devils," he muttered. "We'll have to watch out for him or he'll get us in hot water yet."

"I should say he had already got us in lukewarm," grunted Don. "Let's not wake them, though," he added, pointing to the Merediths, who were still fast asleep.

I spent the next five minutes wondering why I had waked just when I did. Two minutes later and I might have been past awakening. I looked at the roof of the cave and saw the little hole. It had not been there before, I was sure. Would the apes be able to make an opening large enough to come through? I determined to keep an ear out for any noises overhead.

The sun rose, and the forest out in front of us took on color. The dense green was flecked with blossoms of red, white and yellow. A slight breeze shook the leaves and a faint rustling sound came to my ears. Somewhere within that green mantle lay the animals that desired our destruction. It was to be a battle to the finish—and yet a battle without a purpose.

In due time the Merediths awoke, and we had our breakfast. The morning wore on without incident. We lay in the shadows of the cave and looked out on the brilliant jungle, almost wishing an ape would show himself to break the monotony.

Mrs. Meredith did not speak of her grief. Eleanor could not be happy with her brother demented and leagued with a band of apes. Don and I missed her companionship. Dr. Grame and Dr. Meredith withdrew to the back of the cave, and sat in silence. We had all exhausted conversation—there was nothing left to talk about. You can't realize what a terrible state this is until you have experienced it.

The sun beat down on the island with vertical rays, and the air in the cave was hot and sultry. Our water supply was fast diminishing; I judged roughly that it would last us through the next day. I knew that we would have to make some effort to escape, and make it soon. The wildest kind of projects kept turning over in my mind, but none was logical.

Don interrupted my train of thought by asking: "How many cartridges have you left?"

I counted the ones remaining in my belt.

"Eleven," I answered, "and six in my gun—seventeen in all. How many have you?"

"Six in my gun and four in my pocket."

"Twenty-seven between us," I groaned. "Enough to hold off just one more attack. We've got to do something, Don."

He nodded, but said nothing.

In the middle of the afternoon Don called me to the barricade. I had been in the rear of the cave trying to sleep, but the sultry air had kept me awake. When I joined Don at the barricade, he pointed toward the woods.

"Do you see those bushes moving?" he asked.

I followed the direction of his extended arm. There was a little clump of bushes on the edge of the jungle; it was evident that something was moving about in it. Then a body appeared. Don raised his gun and asked almost pleadingly:

"Shall I shoot?"

"No," answered Dr. Meredith, who had joined us. "I think it is coming this way. Wait and see what it does."

It came on toward us through the underbrush. We did not

get a good look at it until it came to the open ground; then we saw it was Nicky.

Dr. Meredith uttered a smothered exclamation, and looked toward Mrs. Meredith, who was sitting in the back of the cave, paying no attention to us.

"Sh-h!" whispered her husband, nodding toward the silent form.

Nicky came on until he was within calling distance. It was obvious he did not want to run any risk of getting caught by us. There were no apes in sight, but I had no doubt that they were waiting in large numbers within the woods, or directly above our heads.

Then he hailed us. His father answered.

"You, mother, sister, and Don will be safe if you surrender. I swear it," called Nicky.

"What about Dr. Grame and Jimmy?" asked Dr. Meredith.

Nicky merely shrugged his shoulders.

Mrs. Meredith had heard Nicky's voice, and rushed to the entrance. She pleaded with him as only a mother can. However, he only laughed. Dr. Meredith realized it would do no good, and only unstring the poor woman's nerves.

"That is not your son, Julia," he said softly, and led her back into the recesses of the cave.

Nicky lingered a while, shouting at us and laughing diabolically.

"We've got to get him away," said Grame. "He'll have the women in hysterics. Plant a shot near him—he'll probably take the hint."

I followed the doctor's suggestion, and a moment later saw Nicky retreating, shaking his fist at us. He disappeared into the green blanket of the hammock, and all was quiet again. The woods sweltered in the heat. We panted for breath.

"He's the funniest one I ever saw," said Don, and I agreed with him.

When Dr. Meredith joined us an idea occurred to me.

"Why don't you give us up?" I asked. "In that case Mrs. Meredith and Eleanor will be safe and—"

"Safe?" said he. "I think not. There is no use discussing it. In the first place I would not consent to abandoning you and Grame. I feel responsible for you—you are my guests, you know," he added with a wan smile. "In the second place, there would be no safety for us among the apes. We are better off as we are."

"Right," answered Grame, and that seemed to settle the matter.

The afternoon dragged on.

"WELL," said Grame, when I had finished unfolding my plan to him, "it might work. I don't see why it shouldn't. At any rate, I agree with you that you ought to try it."

"If we get out of this we're going to have to run some danger any way you look at it," I said.

"Right," he answered. "Go to it, and God help you!"

The afternoon had passed and night come on. All were asleep except Grame and I, who were keeping watch.

I sat a moment looking at the jungle with the tops of the trees lit up by the moonlight, and dark shadows beneath. In a moment I was going to crawl into the night. My return would mean safety for us all; but I might never return.

I did not look forward to the adventure, for I had had enough lately. However, here was a duty to be done, and I was the one to do it, in view of the fact that it was my idea. And so I was ready enough. If I should be caught in the attempt I was about to make, I would die miserably; but if I did not make the attempt, we would probably all die, no less miserably. And so you see, after all, it took no great amount of bravery to steel me for the undertaking.

"I won't take a revolver," I said, "if I'm caught I can kill only a few at the most, and you will have one less gun here. I'll only take my knife."

Grame said no word, but grasped my hand.

"Farewell," he said.

"Just a moment," I muttered, "I want to see whether Eleanor is awake."

"I understand," said my friend. "I'm going to watch the woods."

I made my way silently to where Eleanor was lying. Her breath came regularly and heavily. I dropped to my knees and listened. She was asleep. Why should I wake her? For a while, at any rate, she was not in a cave surrounded by bloodthirsty apes, but in the blessed fields and gardens of dreams. I rose to go, but a hand was laid on my arm.

"I'm not asleep, and I heard you and Dr. Grame."

"I came to say good-by," I said simply.

"Oh, Jimmy," she whispered. "Don't go!"

"Why not?" I asked.

"Because," she answered, "because"— and was silent.

I felt her arms go around my neck, and heard her say: "Because—this—"

The next moment I crushed her in my embrace and kissed her. I held her a moment and then withdrew my arms.

"Do you remember that day when you found me on the raft?" she asked.

I admitted that I did.

"And do you remember that you carried me in your arms?"

"Yes," I answered.

"And do you remember that you did what you did?"

"Yes," I murmured, "I'm sorry, but—"

"Well," she said. "I was conscious all the time."

Such are the ways of woman.

A few moments later Grame lowered the barricade for me and I crawled out into the night as happy as I had ever been in my life.

CHAPTER XIV

CAPTURED!

AS I CREPT toward the dark forest there came a sinking sensation about my heart. How futile the attempt seemed! What chance was there of success in an effort to steal the apes' boats from their own camp?

If I were successful in this, there was every probability that the rest of the plan would miscarry. Would I be able to take the boats to the entrance of the little stream that led up to the pool? How could I bring them all at once, especially if they did not have ropes by which to tow them? I might bring one, and set the rest adrift. But this was counting my chickens before they were hatched, and I turned my thoughts to more immediate problems.

The first thing was to find the camp of the apes. I might happen upon it in ten minutes, and it might take me hours. My best move was to get a view of the whole island from a tall tree, as it was quite probable that the monkeys would have a fire. In that case the first part of my problem would be solved.

There was either no guard on the ledge or he had failed to see me. I made the first fringe of the jungle in safety. It was a far more comfortable feeling to slide along in the deep shadows of the great trees than to inch along through low grass and bushes in the full light of the moon. I felt comparatively secure, so I made the best time I could.

In the course of a few minutes I came upon a tree that suited my purpose very well. The ascent of the trunk to the first branch was difficult enough, but thereafter it was simple. I swung myself up from branch to branch until I was as near the top as my weight made safe.

Clinging to the trunk, with my feet in the forks of two small limbs, I could see over to my left the white crescent of sand that marked the island on which we had first made the acquaintance of our present enemies. Not far from the beach lay Small Island, where I had landed after my journey from Devil's Island. I could even see the latter, an indistinct blotch in the distance.

Below me the hammock lay still as death. The moon lit up the face of the cliff, and a white stretch of shore shone between the black of the forest and gray of the ocean. There was no trace of a fire in any direction. But somewhere below me was the camp of the animals that so closely resembled humans.

Not far distant was a splotch of shadow on the tops of the trees, which stretched away toward the shore in a thin line. I guessed this was the pool and the creek that joined it to the ocean. I strained my eyes in vain for details in the moon-lit tree-tops that might give a clue to the position of the camp I was seeking.

Disappointed by my failure to find anything, I tried to reason out the logical camp site for the apes. I was forced to give it up, as ape reasoning proved baffling.

When I had descended I turned my steps toward the pool. I intended to follow the creek to the ocean and make a tour of the entire shore of the island. The boats would have to be somewhere near the water.

It was extremely difficult to keep any idea of direction. Overhead all was dark, except here or there where the stars or moon peeped through. I found my best guide was the moon, of which I had an occasional glimpse.

Eventually I found myself at the pool, black and still in the shadow of the live oaks and mangroves.

I made my way with difficulty down the bank of the creek

to the shore, and started up the beach, seeking shelter under the fringe of palm trees.

I had walked a half mile or so when a low noise came to my ears. It was a sort of moaning. I had never heard a sound quite like it, so I attributed it to the apes. It seemed to come from up the beach.

Now that I had some clue as to the position of the monkeys' camp the sense of hopelessness that I had experienced before vanished. I advanced cautiously up the shore, listening to the strange noise. It was unquestionably becoming louder and louder, but it was impossible to say whether it came from close at hand or from afar.

Our old camping ground was passed. The sight of it recalled many memories, among others those of a water barrel.

The noise now seemed to be coming from inland. I pushed through a thick screen of vines, stopped short, and crouched down. In front of me was what I sought.

The apes were there! They were all on their bellies, squirming about the ground, and uttering the peculiar sound that had led me to them. As I watched I began to realize that there was some method in the mad wriggling. The prone forms seemed to be crawling in concentric circles. In the center was a figure seated majestically on a block of wood and holding a baton in its hand. In the moonlight I recognized Nicky.

After a while the apes ceased wriggling along the ground and formed themselves into a line, standing. The line approached the sitting figure. The first one knelt in front of Nicky. The boy rose, and after uttering a few gibberish sounds, tapped the ape on the head with his stick. This performance was repeated with each one of the monkeys. I suppose it was some sort of coronation ceremony to celebrate the accession of the new king.

Nothing could have fitted in better with my design to get possession of the boats. All the apes were presumably engrossed in the fete; it would be easy to pass unnoticed, for they had eyes and ears for nothing but their strange rites.

I guessed that the boats were nearby on the beach, probably made fast to stumps or logs. I advanced along the edge of the clearing, keeping close to the tree trunks. The shadows hid me well. However, my very caution proved to be my undoing. As I hugged the tree trunks I pushed into one that had been dead for a long time.

It must have been on the point of falling, for my weight sufficed to topple it over. Down it came, ripping through the branches of the neighboring trees, and hit the ground with a crash. I looked hurriedly toward the apes; they had ceased their ceremony, and were gazing in the direction of the fallen tree. Then they started to advance, slowly at first, and then more rapidly. It was evident that their suspicions had been aroused.

There was still time to escape in the darkness, but haste was imperative. I started off, gliding as rapidly as possible from tree to tree. Luckily the ground was open. The apes must have heard me, for they began to run. I followed their lead and set out at full speed.

But luck was against me. My toe caught in a root, and I went flying into a thicket. I must have hit a tree trunk, for I felt a stunning blow on the head, and lost consciousness.

I do not know how long I lay thus. When I came to it seemed

to me that a large hammer was striking rhythmically on the back of my head. I could still hear my pursuers beating the woods for me. At times they passed so close I could hear their low chattering.

I must have lost consciousness again. When I came to, the second time, all was silent. The apes must have given me up, I thought. Getting to my feet dizzily I determined to continue my search for the boats. I felt myself fainting once or twice, and had to sit down.

There was a thick mass of vines ahead of me, and I thought I had better not try to push through it in my present state. As I skirted the edge, an arm was passed around my neck from behind, and I was dragged backward in a powerful embrace.

I struggled fiercely and tried to reach my knife; but to no avail. The hold around my neck tightened and I could not breathe. My knees began to sag, and the hands that tore at the hairy arm had no strength. Then all went black, and I knew no more.

THE NEXT thing I remembered was a very uncomfortable feeling. For some reason or other I could not move my legs and arms. I tried to rub my head, but could not. For what seemed a long time I wondered where I was, and what was the matter. Then my thoughts cleared, and I found myself tied firmly to a tree. My head ached, and my strength seemed to have left me. This, then, was the end of my attempt to save Eleanor and the others. It had been a poor attempt, and luck had played me into the apes' hands. I wondered if the ones back in the cave were still safe.

Several yards in front of me lay four or five sleeping simians. Where were the rest? I could only guess. Perhaps they were storming the cave; perhaps they had already stormed it, and all my friends were dead or captives. And so my thoughts ran along in unpleasant channels.

Although I was tied in a trying position, I sank into fitful dozes, partly because of fatigue, partly because of weakness resulting from the blow on my head. In one of my waking moments I wondered why they had not killed me at once. They did not wish to be rid of me; they were reserving me for torture.

I was still shuddering at the thought, when I heard the leaves behind me rustling. The noise persisted; then I thought I heard footsteps, soft and stealthy. They became distinct; some one was approaching, slowly, cautiously. Each foot was planted with care and several seconds lapsed between each step.

Was it one of the apes? Was it Nicky, coming to have his revenge on me? I started to call out to my sleeping guards, but reconsidered. The steps were coming very near.

I gave a tremendous wrench in order to turn my body enough to catch a glimpse of the unknown.

"Be quiet, for God's sake!" whispered a voice. "It's I, Don."

In a moment his hand was feeling for my knife, with which to cut the creepers that bound me.

CHAPTER XV

THE FLIGHT IN THE JUNGLE

QUIETLY WE CREPT away toward the shore, with a great fear of awakening the sleeping apes. As soon as we were out of earshot I asked Don: "How did you happen to find me?"

"Eleanor," he answered. "When you didn't turn up after four hours, she swore she was going to look for you. We persuaded her to let me do it in her place."

I was too deeply moved to speak for several moments. She loved me! She was willing to risk herself in a dark jungle full of savage apes—for me! It made me feel very much ashamed. I was too foolish, too careless, to deserve such consideration.

Don broke my chain of thoughts by telling me he had found the boats, dragged up on the beach a little above our old camping place. We had been walking in that direction; in five minutes we should be there. I was weak, and was glad to let Don help me over the fallen trees and make a way for me among the vines and creepers. There was a large bump on my forehead where I had connected with a trunk or root when I fell into the thicket.

The moon, peeping in through the thick screen of leaves now and then, lighted up out path fitfully. I judged it would set-in a couple of hours. If we could only make our get-away while the light lasted! After we were in the boats darkness would be to our advantage.

The hammock became less dense, and we could hear the noise of the waves. The coast was not far away. We crept along to the edge of the forest and saw a dark group of boats.

As we advanced Don poked me and said: "Do you see anything by the boats?"

I looked and saw an ape on guard.

"Wonder if there are any more about besides that one?" muttered Don.

"Let's scout around and see," I suggested. "If the guard is the only one, we ought to be able to make short work of him."

We slid along under the trees among the shadows until we were opposite the rude canoes. There were no signs of any other apes.

"Give me your knife," said Don, "and you take the gun. I'll try to get him with this. Don't shoot unless you have to."

"All right," I answered. "Go ahead. I'll follow and shoot if necessary."

The ape was sitting in one of the boats, looking out to sea, with his back toward us. Don started to creep over the soft sand to the still form; a twig snapped under him, and we fell flat. As we lay on the ground the sentinel turned his head, but did not see us. After the lapse of a minute Don motioned to me, and we resumed our advance.

The sea stretched away darkly, except where the moon drew a smear of light across it. The ape's silhouette showed faintly against the horizon.

We had come very close now. I had stopped, while Don was inching along the sand on his belly. I scarcely dared breathe and felt the guard must hear his enemy's approach. The leaves rustled in the breeze and the waves lapped the shore ceaselessly.

Don was at the boat. I saw him rise ghostlike from the sand; the knife shone in the moonlight. Then came two quick flashes, and the ape sank with a groan. I hastened up and helped Don drag the thing out of the boat.

"Confound it!" muttered my companion. "No paddles! They must have hidden them."

A hurried search failed to bring them to light. However, we

did find a tree limb, and an old board that must have floated in from some wrecks These would serve the purpose, and we hadn't any time to lose. We returned to the boats.

"Two will be enough for us," said Don. "Shall we try to tow the rest and set them adrift?"

"The wind's blowing inshore, and they would probably get washed up on the island if we cast them loose. We had better take them with us."

There were four canoes altogether, and none had painters of any sort. How to tow them was the problem.

"Guess we'll have to use our clothes," I said resignedly.

"No; I have another idea," said Don. "We'll use some of those confounded vines we've been tripping over ever since we landed on this island."

In a short time we had cut several tough, pliant creepers, and had the boats launched and tied up in a line ready for departure. Our progress was slow and laborious. The canoes were heavy, and the makeshift paddles were far from efficient.

Time rolled by slowly as we sweated over our boards. It seemed hours before we arrived at the creek. The moon was getting low, and we had little time to act. The boats were towed into the mouth of the stream and made fast to the trees on the bank.

"Shall we both go for the people, or had one of us better stay here?" asked Don.

I thought it would be better for one to stay with the boats, and told him my opinion.

"Then you go, and I'll stay," he answered with a smile.

"I'll try not to be away long," I replied, as I started up the bank of the creek.

Things were turning out well, after all, I thought, as I walked toward the cave. We had the boats; if I could only get the people in the cave to the shore before the apes turned up, we would be saved. What we would do after we made our escape did not enter my mind.

I passed the pool, and then came to the edge of the wood in front of the cave. No guard was visible on the ledge above, so I went straight to the entrance. Grame and Eleanor let down the barricade for me. Dr. and Mrs. Meredith had been awakened the moment Grame had seen me approaching, and were ready for the arduous trip to the coast.

I briefly recounted my adventures, and we started out for the creek, carrying only the few cans of food that were left and the almost empty water cask.

I went first with Eleanor, then came the Merediths, and Grame brought up the rear. Our progress was slow, for the jungle with its tangle of branches, vines and creepers proved difficult for Mrs. Meredith. Her strength was below normal, because of the hardship of life in the cave, and her grief over the loss of Nicky.

"Just think," I whispered to Eleanor as I helped her over a fallen tree, "in ten minutes we will be safe. In half an hour we will have left this land behind."

"And Nicky, too," she added, and her voice caught.

I had not thought of that side of it before. Of course it would be hard for the Merediths to leave their child behind in the midst of a band of wild animals. True, he ruled them now, but might they not turn on him some time—especially if he should have another change and become himself again?

"Don't worry," I answered, and took her hand. "We won't go far. As soon as you and your mother are out of danger, Grame and I will come back for Nicky. We got him once; we can do it again."

My hand was gripped tightly in reply. However, my confidence in our ability to kidnap Nicky from the apes was not as great as I tried to paint it. I knew there was still a great deal of uncertainty and danger before us; especially in this last enterprise that had so suddenly been called to my attention. It was a duty, and would have to be undertaken. No one knew how sick I was becoming of tropical islands and adventure.

When we came to the pool we stopped to rest a while. Dr. Grame and I did a little scouting while the others got their breath, but found no traces of the apes.

In the course of a few minutes we were on our way again, traveling down the right bank of the creek. The jungle was so thick that Mrs. Meredith found it almost impossible to walk. Dr. Grame suggested that if we got farther away from the water the undergrowth would be less dense. We acted upon his advice and found that he was right. So we made our way toward the sea, parallel to the creek but at a distance of about a hundred yards from it.

When we suddenly came out of the forest onto the sandy beach, and the ocean before us lay polished by the slanting rays of the disappearing moon, a little cry of gratitude escaped Eleanor.

"The boats are just a little way up the beach," I said, restraining my joy with difficulty.

We had not advanced three steps when Don appeared ahead. I waved my hand to him, and he waved back. Then he stopped suddenly and peered intently into the woods. Almost immediately he fell on his stomach and made signs to us to go back into the hammock.

His actions struck fear into my heart, and I divined what was afoot even before I saw two brown forms emerge from the forest opposite Don. They were followed by others.

"My God!" cried Grame. "We are just too late."

"No, we aren't," I said. "Remember we still have our guns."

"But only twenty-seven cartridges," he rejoined. "Let's wait and see how many there are before we advance."

It was soon apparent that there were too many for us. I judged there must have been fifty present.

"Let's try to frighten them," I suggested. "If we killed a few they might run."

"I doubt it," answered Grame, "but we can try."

So we started to run up the beach.

"Wait," said Grame, before we had gone fifteen feet. "One of us has got to stay with the women. There may be more of them in the woods there, and they could attack the Merediths undefended."

"You stay," I answered. "You can take care of them better than I."

With that I started up the beach again. More apes were coming out of the woods. I could see two of them advancing upon Don. I rushed on to help him, but several apes intervened. I saw him strike with his knife. One of his opponents fell, while he grappled with the other. Three big fellows rushed at me, but I shot them down and passed on.

Then Don got up. He had evidently killed his second opponent. He started toward me, but it was evident we could not reach each other. At least thirty apes were between us.

"The boats!" I howled at Don. "You try to make the boats."

"All right," he called. "I'll go to Small Island. Back soon."

He set out up the beach at full speed. As for me, I shot two more apes, but they did not seem to be at all awed.

Most of them had started in pursuit of Don, but seven or eight were now rapidly coming toward me. Realizing I could not hold them all, I turned and ran toward the party that were awaiting me. I had presence of mind enough to reload my revolver as I went.

Fortunately the apes were not very fast, so I reached the others well in advance of my pursuers.

"We'll have to take to the woods and try to get back to the cave," said Grame. "There's no time to lose."

He was right, and we started for the forest as rapidly as we could.

CHAPTER XVI

AN AWFUL PROSPECT

AS WE PUSHED our way through the hammock, the noise of the pursuit was in our ears. We would be able to stop one or two attacks, but after our ammunition had been exhausted our only safety would be the cave.

"Lucky for us most of them went after Don," said Grame. "I suppose they figure we are cornered; I almost believe they are right."

I shall not go into the details of that flight. There was no stopping for rest at the pool; there was not even a let-up in our pace. We ran across small bands of our pursuers twice; each time their attacks were repulsed with losses for them.

At last Mrs. Meredith's endurance gave way. She could go no farther.

"We are almost there, dear," said Dr. Meredith. "Rest a moment, and then we will reach the cave in a few minutes."

In truth, the cave was near; we were almost at the edge of the jungle. The rest was welcome to us, for the flight from the coast had been rapid and exhausting. I can't understand how the women stood up the way they did. It was one of the bravest things I have ever witnessed.

"Look!" whispered Grame to me, pointing to the right.

The trees were less dense in that direction. I caught fleeting glimpses of a band of apes loping through the jungle.

"We can't be cut off just at the last moment again," hissed Grame. "Lie still!"

We warned the others and lay perfectly quiet. The dark forms could still be seen moving along with their peculiar walk. However, they were going away from us. The sight of this queer band threading through the jungle fascinated me. I kept my eyes glued on them. Presently I had a feeling of uneasiness, a feeling that all was not right. Instinctively I glanced around with apprehension. It was well I did. Out of the high sedge grass beside which Grame was lying there appeared a hand, clutching a knife. It hovered above the doctor's back.

With a spring forward I seized the arm as it descended, and gave a violent jerk. The knife was dropped, and the small figure of Nicky came tumbling out of the grass.

Before he could utter a cry I fell upon him and clapped my hand over his mouth. He struggled violently for several moments, but soon realized the futility of his exertions.

Grame improvised a gag from his handkerchief and a twig, and applied it to Nicky's mouth. A belt sufficed to make the boy's arms fast behind his back. Then we lay down again and waited for several minutes, to give the band of apes ample time to get out of earshot.

When Grame thought we had allowed sufficient time, the party was set in motion again, and after a short, uneventful walk we arrived at the lowered barricade in front of the cave.

"Better find out whether anything is in there, first," suggested Dr. Meredith.

Grame entered with his gun raised, and we heard him walking about. Then he called out:

"All right. Come in. No apes here."

INSIDE, we deposited Nicky on the ground. He insisted on lying on his stomach, and we could see little of his face. However, the few glances we did get showed us that he still had that bestiality of expression that characterized his periods of lapse. His mother tried to talk to him, but to no avail. He either could not or would not speak.

"Better not untie him," said Grame. "He may give us the slip again."

The mother in Mrs. Meredith was inclined to protest, but her common sense was strong, so she acquiesced. She kept Nicky beside her, and soon he was apparently asleep. Dr. Meredith suggested that we follow suit and gain strength for the next day.

It would have been out of reason to dispense with a guard, so I volunteered to take the first turn. The moon had long set, and only the stars were left to shed their light over the gloomy scene in front of us. As I viewed our position in my mind's eye the aspect was far from cheerful. No food, no water. The last remnant of each had been abandoned in our flight back from the shore.

Only six cartridges were left; hardly enough to repulse an attack in the cave. Fortunately the possibility of such an attack was small for some time. The apes had had too many unfortunate experiences before the barricade to attempt it again soon; besides, they had lost their leader.

But what were we to do? Suppose the apes did not attack us. We could live possibly for two or three days in the torture of hunger and thirst. It was evident that there was only one way for us; we would have to steal our way to the coast and swim for it. If we could leave the island unseen our chances of life would be good.

I heard a step beside me, and looked up to see Eleanor. She sat down on the ground and we looked out at the night together.

"Nice mess, isn't it?" she said with a little laugh. "I used to read of adventure in books, and wanted it. I don't think so much of it now."

"I could get along without any more of it myself," I answered.

We were silent a moment. It was wonderful how lightly this girl could talk of our position, when she knew that our lives were in the balance. After all, it was the only way to keep up our courage.

"How about water?" Eleanor asked.

"There isn't any," I had to admit. "The cask was left behind when we ran back here."

"Well, there wasn't much in it, anyway," she said bravely.

"Are you thirsty?" I asked.

"Not yet," was her prophetic reply. It made me shudder.

What horrors of thirst might be in store for us among these green islands, sweltering under the direct rays of the tropical sun?

"What are we going to do?"

For the first time there seemed to be a quaver in her voice.

"Oh, we'll manage well enough," I tried to be reassuring. "I should think the thing to do would be to try to get to the coast to-morrow night and swim to some near-by island. We could keep swimming from one to another, and perhaps be picked up before the apes found us again."

"Is there any fresh water on these islands?" she asked.

"Don't believe so," I replied. "Guess we'll have to ruin our digestions forever by drinking coconut milk."

And then we sat quiet, each harboring his own horrible thoughts. Mental pictures of long, broiling days without water, and fatiguing night swims from one small mosquito infested isle to another. But we kept such thoughts to ourselves and spoke lightly enough.

At length Eleanor interrupted the silence by saying:

"I wonder where Don is? Do you suppose he got away all right?"

In answer I drew from my belt the knife I had wrenched from Nicky, and laid it before her.

"What do you mean?" she demanded, although no doubt she guessed the truth.

"When I left Don at the boats he had this. When he fought the apes on the shore he had it. I saw it gleam in the moonlight.

And yet that is the knife Nicky nearly ended Grame with back in the forest."

"You mean—" she said, with a catch in her voice.

"Yes, I'm afraid so. How else could Nicky have gotten the knife? There is a possibility Don dropped it—but he probably didn't."

"Poor Don!" she murmured. "He was a brave boy."

"He certainly was," I answered. "Perhaps he still is. He may have escaped."

She did not reply.

One more of our party gone. Who would be the next?

Youth, however, is by nature optimistic. If it weren't, we would all go to a crossroads grave early in life. In spite of our danger, there was something inside us both that whispered: "Oh, we'll get through this all right." The idea of getting back home turned my thoughts in a different channel.

"Eleanor," I said, taking her hand, "we will probably all get home safely. If we do, I'm going to ask you something before we have been there long. It would be unfair to do it here amid all this adventure and danger. Things might look different in a different climate."

Her answer was to put her arms around my neck and lay her cheek against mine.

"Things will never look different to me so far as you are concerned," she said. "You have been tested rather thoroughly out here."

A little while later Eleanor went to the back of the cave and went to sleep beside her mother.

The hours wore on in cool darkness. I wanted to watch until daylight. However, my eyelids kept closing against my will, and I caught myself nodding time after time. I realized that I could not keep awake much longer, so rather than run a risk of having our party unguarded I roused Grame, who swore because I had not called him earlier. Inside of three minutes I sank into a dreamless slumber

CHAPTER XVII

THE LAST STAND

WHEN I AWOKE the cave was light; the dazzle of the sun in the entrance blinded my eyes. All the rest were awake, sitting down and doing nothing as far as I could see.

"Good morning, all," I said in a voice thick with sleep.

They looked up and answered my salutation. The faces appeared more cheerful than I had seen them for a long time. I felt that something had happened which favored us.

"What's the good word?" I asked. "What do you all look so happy about?"

"Me, I suppose," answered Nicky with a shamed expression. "I'm all right again."

"Fine!" I said.

"I wish I could stay this way," he continued wistfully. "Please don't think I'm bad 'cause I want to be. I can't help it—I really can't."

He burst into sobs, hiding his face against his mother's bosom.

"There, there, precious!" cooed his mother. "It's all right. It's a kind of sickness. We'll take care of you, and you will get over it."

Mrs. Meredith restrained her own tears with difficulty, and there was a catch in her voice. Something tugged in my throat, too. It was truly a pitiful scene, this contrite little boy who wanted to be good, but whom nature forced to be a beast.

Grame took me by the arm, indicating that we should leave

the child and mother alone. We walked to the entrance and leaned against the rocky side of the cave. I noticed that the sun was high, and guessed it was about eleven o'clock.

"Quite a bit has happened while you were asleep," said my companion. "Nicky returned to normal some time during the night and was quite himself this morning. I did some thinking last night, and it now seems to me our only hope is to get to the coast and swim to one of the neighboring islands. If we kept a good lookout we could keep hidden from the apes indefinitely."

"Just my idea," I agreed.

"Well," he continued, "among other things I learned from Nicky was the fact that Don was not killed. He escaped. The apes found the knife left in one of their comrades that Don had killed. Don was either unable or hadn't time to loosen it.

"At any rate, he reached his boat and shoved off before the apes reached the mouth of the stream. The apes had no paddles, and can't swim, so Nicky says, so Don escaped. If we can only find him, everything will be fine. But it will be hard, because he will be hiding from the apes, and consequently from us also, although he doesn't know it."

"He went to Small Island," I answered.

"Which one is that—the little one next to us?" asked Grame.

"Yes," I replied.

"How do you know?"

"As he ran for the boats he called the name to me."

"Good!" said Grame. "We'll give these apes the slip yet."

"How do you think the chances are of our getting to the shore?" I asked at length.

"Pretty good," replied Grame. "If the apes do run across us, Nicky is going to put on a stiff front and pretend we are his captives. He will use his authority as grand chief, and arrange some way for us all to escape. However, I don't see why we can't make the coast without being caught."

The hours dragged by monotonously. Our lunch consisted

of a can of beans that Eleanor had kept throughout the flight of last night. Dr. Meredith had also clung to a can he carried, and after lunch there was one can of beans between us and starvation.

We had no water at all, but as yet no one was actually suffering. However, it was easy to see what our future would be if we didn't make our escape that night. We had to leave the cave very soon, or experience the horrors of slow death from thirst.

"We want to start soon after dark, before the moon comes up," said Grame. "The less light, the better for us."

"Hadn't we better wait till the apes are asleep?" suggested Dr. Meredith. "We might run across a party of them scouting for food or something."

"It strikes me that we run a better chance with no moon, even if the apes are awake. They wouldn't be likely to be wandering around in the dark," answered Grame.

"I guess you are right," admitted Dr. Meredith.

About an hour after twilight had vanished Grame suggested it was a good time to start. All agreed, and we were getting ready to lower the barricade when Nicky intervened.

"Wait a minute," said the child. "What about the guard above the entrance?"

"Is there one?" gasped Grame.

"Yes," said Nicky. "Didn't you know it?"

"No," muttered the doctor, "That changes matters."

"I have an idea," said Nicky. "The guard is instructed to give the alarm if any one tries to leave, but if Eleanor goes out he is to try to capture her without making any noise. Now, if we let her go out, the guard will probably try to get her. Why don't we pretend to be asleep and let Eleanor stand under the ledge. We could stay near and see what happens. You might get a chance to kill him without shooting."

This struck me as a good but dangerous plan. However, I hoped that Nicky wasn't getting ready for another lapse. It seemed to me his mind was running in a cunning track.

Grame looked at Eleanor.

"I'm willing," she replied shortly.

"Good!" said Grame. "It's our best bet. Don't worry, we won't let him hurt you, even if we have to shoot."

We let down the barricade shortly, and Eleanor slipped out. Grame and I stood ready, he with his revolver and I with the knife. The girl stood in front of the entrance silent and stiff. Several minutes passed.

"Do you suppose he is there?" whispered Grame.

His answer was a shuffling noise from overhead, faint but audible. Several seconds more passed, and a dark body shot down. It landed on Eleanor and bore her to the ground.

In a trice I was above the brute and had stabbed him in the neck several times. With a little rattling noise he rolled over on his side and lay stiffly silent. Eleanor regained her feet alone and with a nervous laugh assured us that she was unhurt.

"I was scared to death, though," she added.

"No wonder," said Grame.

And so we started out on our second attempt to escape. As we made our tedious way through the difficult tangle, Eleanor walked with me. It was a great comfort to be with her; her spirits never flagged once, and she did not permit the least doubt of the outcome of our adventure to enter her mind.

Mrs. Meredith also had been greatly aided both in strength and spirit by Nicky's return and recovery. She was quite cheerful and bore up well. Dr. Grame assisted her while Dr. Meredith gave Nicky a helping hand.

Instead of going toward the pool and then down the creek to the shore, we struck off at right angles. This course, although longer, would enable us to strike the beach just at the point where it was nearest Small Island. Besides, the jungle was much denser in this direction. While difficult to traverse, it provided far more protection. It was an ideal place to hide.

After we had pushed forward about an hour, Grame called a halt for a general rest.

"The shore can't be much farther away," I said.

"I believe you're right," said the doctor. "At any rate, I hope so." And he laughed.

We were getting so near safety that every one in the party was in a good humor. We indulged in joking for almost the first time since we had reached the island.

When Grame suggested that we move on again, all responded cheerfully. As we advanced, the ground became more open, and progress was considerably more rapid and easy. However, as I walked along, engrossed in pleasant thoughts of the future, a feeling of uneasiness crept upon me. Try as I would, I could not refrain from casting backward glances over my shoulder. What was it that gave me this feeling of alarm? I could not say.

A pale glow in the eastern sky announced the early advent of the moon. Perhaps it was the ghostlike sheet of light that filled me with foreboding. At all events, I soon noticed that Grame also appeared nervous. All our gayety was now gone. We ought to be at the shore in fifteen minutes or so, I judged. Would to God it would be a short quarter hour!

At length Grame held up his hand and called us to a halt. He looked at me interrogatively, and listened intently. I followed his example, and yet I heard nothing but the whispering of the breeze in the foliage.

"Hear anything?" asked Grame.

"No," I answered.

We took up our way again, but with an eye and an ear ever to the rear. No more smiles—we went forward as quickly as we possibly could. The shore was near.

An intermittent crackling to our rear began to be audible. It grew louder rapidly and was soon noticed by every one. "The apes?" whispered Dr. Meredith. Grame nodded affirmatively and urged us to make all speed. The moon was now lighting up the forest and we could see our way. The tangle had altogether disappeared and the trees were getting less dense. These were signs that the ocean was near, and I took heart. On we plunged toward safety and the shore.

"Wait!" called Nicky. "I hear something ahead."

We stopped, precious as time was.

"Hear that?" demanded the child, as a noise of breaking twigs came to us.

"It's from the rear," said Grame.

"It's not," insisted Nicky. "It's ahead of us."

We listened again. The child was right—the noise was coming from ahead.

"Hell," muttered the doctor. After a pause he added: "Let's go on, anyway. If we can break through them and make the sea, we are all right; they can't swim, and haven't their boats with them."

"They must have," said Dr. Meredith, "else how could they be coming toward us? They must have paddled around and left their boats on the beach ahead."

"Guess you're right," admitted Grame. "At any rate, they have cut us off. However, we might as well go on."

And on we went, but with our hearts in our boots. To be cut off just as escape was in our grasp! It was heart-breaking. I did not know whether to curse or cry; I felt like doing both.

While the apes ahead were still a good way off, the ones from the rear came into view, slipping among the trees silently like ghosts. In the course of a minute or so they would be upon us in force.

"It's up to you, Nicky," said Grame to the child as we came to a halt. "See what you can do with them. You're chief, you know."

The child walked several paces toward the apes and halted. We stood in a little group where we were. The apes approached slowly, grouping together as they came. At length some forty of them stood before the small, erect figure.

When they had all arrived Nicky began to chatter at them.

The apes listened in silence for a while; however, they seemed to be getting worked up. Their cold passivity of posture changed to a nervous shifting. At length one of them broke in and chattered angrily. Others joined, but were silenced by Nicky and the ape spokesman. The chattering continued and became more heated. The apes were crowding closer to Nicky and some of them were eying us fiercely.

One big black fellow made a break and came lunging toward us. A shriek from Eleanor caused Nicky to turn his head. When he saw what was happening he snatched a small stick from his blouse and with two quick steps stood in the path of the rushing ape, who stopped a moment and then brushed Nicky aside. With a quick movement the child struck him with the wand directly on the head.

A loud roar came from the band in front of us. As one they rushed upon the black ape and bore him to the ground. Then a struggling, snarling mass was all that was visible.

Nicky came toward us.

"Now's our chance," called Grame.

"No," commanded Nicky. "Don't you see those not fighting—they would give the alarm. Besides, I think we are safe now. This"—tapping the wand—"is the chiefs emblem. It touches the head of each ape when the chief is first made. After that, any ape whose head it touches is torn to pieces by the others. It is a custom they are afraid to break, for some reason."

The apes were now getting back to their feet. A mass of bloody hair and flesh lay where the black ape had fallen. The sight made me shudder. I wondered what I would look like if they decided to treat me the same way.

Nicky took his post a little ahead of us. A large ape approached him, while the others kept their distance.

While Nicky and the ape chattered at each other I heard the other party coming close and closer. They would reach us in a minute at the most. The chattering grew hot. The ape began to scream; his shrill voice rose higher and higher. Then he turned and made a sign to the others. They began to advance, cautiously, however.

"Watch out!" yelled Nicky to us, and struck at the ape with his wand. The ape was too quick, and seized the stick from Nicky's clutch. Pushing the child aside, he advanced toward us.

Then Nicky did a very brave thing. Sneaking up behind the great ape, he snatched the wand from his unsuspecting grasp. But before he could strike, the ape also grasped the wand again, and the two closed in a grapple. Mrs. Meredith screamed, while the apes rushed forward. Grame's revolver spoke, and the ape released Nicky, but held tenaciously to the wand.

"Come to us! Leave the stick!" cried Grame hoarsely.

But Nicky would not. Instead, he made a lunge for the little piece of wood, in a last effort to save our lives. But the other apes were too near, and trampled him down. In a moment they were upon us.

Fortunately we were in a circle, and our fire proved effective. The first charge was checked. As the apes collected their force for a second rush Eleanor whispered in my ear:

"For God's sake, shoot me with the last cartridge! Promise!"

I promised, and kissed the hand she held out. Then the rush came, and I knew all was over. We couldn't check this one. I fired one shot—there was one left. I turned toward Eleanor. But my finger refused to pull the trigger. Instead, I handed her the gun, and said:

"You may escape yet—"

A body crashed into me. I sank my knife into it. Then I struck out again and again. Something hit my head; my knees gave way and I sank to the ground. Then I heard the explosion of a gun—she had killed herself!

That meant the end of the world for me. Another shot came, and then many. Was I mad? I decided I was, for we had had only one bullet left between us. I attributed the other shots to delirium as I sank into unconsciousness.

CHAPTER XVIII

THE MYSTERIOUS ISLE

WHEN I WENT down beneath the apes I never thought to see the light of day again; so as I recovered from the dark void in which I had lain and began to feel and think, I supposed I was dead. My dazed brain was playing me odd tricks, and I wondered if this was how everybody else felt after death. Strangely enough, my memory was perfectly good. All the events of the last few days were arrayed in my mind as clearly cut as photographs—the fight with the shark, the trouble with the apes, our last stand, and the death of Eleanor and myself.

I seemed to be lying on my back, and my head was pillowed on something soft. Nevertheless, it throbbed and throbbed, no doubt because of a blow one of the apes had dealt me. My eyelids fluttered cautiously and I peered forth into the semi-darkness.

A face was dimly visible above me, and when my eyes had become accustomed to the gloom I saw that it was Eleanor's. For a moment I forgot that I was dead, and felt perfectly natural. Then a wave of dizziness swept over me.

I remembered that Eleanor and I were both among those who had departed from the earth, and were together, as was fitting, somewhere in the next world. My head was pillowed in her lap, and she was stroking my forehead.

Catching her eye, I muttered inquiringly: "Heaven?"

Eleanor smiled and shook her head.

"West Indies," she said; then asked pityingly: "How do you feel?"

Disregarding her solicitude, I mumbled: "But you're dead. Shot yourself. I heard you."

"No, Jimmy," replied my vision. "Don fired that shot at the apes."

"Then we're alive?" I questioned feebly.

"Yes," she nodded brightly.

And then thinking of the apes—the danger—I attempted to bound to my feet. My knees gave way, and I fell back reeling.

"There, there!" soothed Eleanor. "Everything is all right. We're quite safe, so make yourself easy."

With that she drew my head back into her lap and set to rubbing my forehead again ever so lightly.

"Tell me what happened," I whispered, consumed with curiosity. "Where are we—Large Island?"

"No," she answered; "we are on a new island—Captain's Island, we call it. You see, Don escaped from the apes last night; he found Captain Johnson and three of his men to-day and brought them to Large Island to-night just in time to save us from the apes. They arrived as you fell, and the shot you heard was not from my gun, but from Don's, and it killed the ape that hit your head. No one was hurt."

As I lay on the sand with my head pillowed in Eleanor's lap, I was filled with a huge sense of rest and contentment. We were temporarily safe from the apes, and all were unharmed. As my head was rapidly ceasing to ache, I began to take note of our surroundings.

It was one of those soft, brilliant nights of which the tropics are rightfully proud, with a big white moon beaming down upon land and sea, and a balmy breeze rustling through the trees. From nearby came the fragrance of the night blooming jasmine and budding orange blossoms, while overhead the big bright stars danced and twinkled. The deathless murmur of the sea constituted the only sound.

As I lay spellbound by the enchantment of the place I watched Eleanor peering out over the gently rolling ocean. Her face, silhouetted against the dark azure of the sky, was bewitchingly beautiful, and as I looked a great feeling of tenderness for her surged over me. Think what the poor girl had been through lately! With a great effort of will I stirred myself from the lethargy of beauty in which I basked, and plied Eleanor with questions concerning our escape.

During the fight with the apes the previous night, when we had been driven from the boats back to our cave, Don had escaped with all the canoes. He made his way safely with them to Small Island. However, it occurred to him that the part of wisdom would be to get the boats farther away, in order that the apes could not recover them. So he paddled to a group of islands some miles to the right, where he found a swift current flowing in the opposite direction from Large Island. Setting all the boats adrift here, save two, he watched them float away in the distance. Then he landed on a nearby island, beached his canoes, and fell asleep.

The next day he awakened late. He intended returning to Large Island that night with two canoes, in an effort to sneak us through the apes to the coast and the boats. So while he was waiting for the darkness to fall he spent his time exploring.

As he made his way westward with the two crazy ape boats, he discovered a man standing on the beach of a neighboring island. A shout brought a reply. It was Captain Johnson.

The captain and three other men of the crew had been cruising around among the different keys in search of the Meredith party. However, they had turned their attention to the northern isles, as these were nearer the wrecked Mermaid, and consequently had missed us.

It was now approaching sunset, so the party collected their arms and ammunition, of which they had plenty, and set out with Don, bent on our rescue. Out of caution they landed on the shore of Large Island that was nearest to Small Island, and began the journey through the hammock toward our cave. Then they heard sounds ahead. At first they believed the apes were in front, and took council as to how to avoid them. However, the captain thought he heard a human voice, and the party dashed forward to investigate.

They reached us just as the apes began their attack. Taken by surprise, many of our enemies were slaughtered by the rain of bullets from the five guns at close range. The shattered remnant of the ape band broke into flight to escape further destruction, and were not pursued.

After we had been rescued, the captain led our party to the boats, and we were rowed to the island on which we now were.

When Eleanor finished recounting the tale I asked:

"Where are the others now?"

Eleanor pointed down the beach.

"Around the bend there," she said. "They left you here with me so you would have rest and quiet."

"By this time I was beginning to feel quite fit, so I gained my feet and wobbled uncertainly. Eleanor supported me till I felt master of my legs, and then we began our journey down the sand.

However, it was not long before I grew tired, and we stopped to rest a moment under a jasmine tree. Now as I stood there, and turned my memory to the adventures and dangers we had safely weathered of late, my mind, aided and abetted by the fragrance of the jasmine and the hum of the huge palm fans shivering under the moon in a slight breeze, allowed itself to be swept by the infinite romance of the night and the tropical island.

Realizing that I loved Eleanor—loved her with all my heart and soul—imprisoned her two hands in mine. She bowed her head a trifle and freed her hands; turning to one side, she absentmindedly plucked a spray of jasmine. Then, as if struck with an idea, she turned, and, smiling sweetly up into my face, made as if to place it in the lapel of my coat—but since I had not a coat on, she drew the stem of the sprays through a buttonhole in my shirt several a inches below my chin.

When this operation had been completed she stood directly before me, with her hands hovering about the nosegay she had just bestowed.

Smiling roguishly through her moonlit eyes, she said:

"You said there was something you wished to say to me when we got home. Isn't this as good as home?"

"I'll *show* you what I had to say," I breathed, and the next moment my arms were filled with loveliness, and her fragrant lips were tightly pressed to mine. In that one moment all the trials and fears of the foregoing days were requited.

After a few seconds she tore away from me and began to run. Then she stopped and seemed to reflect.

Turning toward me with a laugh, she said:

"When a girl is kissed for the first time, it is fitting that she should run away. But this is not the first time you have kissed me, so give me your arm, and we will walk to meet the others in a sensible manner."

As I thought of the circumstances under which I had first kissed the lovely girl at my side, I blushed slightly and laughed. The island episode seemed very amusing now.

As we walked arm and arm along the beach, with the waves bubbling on the sand, I was very happy. Turning abruptly to Eleanor, I said:

"Honey, I've told you I love you. Do you love me enough to marry me?"

"Of course, foolish," she answered. "I thought we were taking that for granted."

So it was with light hearts that we both I walked on in silence till the light of a fire flashed into view from behind some trees. Then some one saw us, and a shout hailed our approach.

"Well again!" boomed Grame's big voice. "Well, you ought to be—we left you with an ideal nurse."

And he broke into a laugh, while the darkness hid my companion's blush.

After greeting the captain and assuring the rest of the company that I was all right, I motioned Grame aside, and asked him:

"Well, how is Nicky?"

"Seems to be all that could be desired right now. However, there is no telling what he will be like to-morrow."

"Tell me, doctor," I asked, "do you think he will ever recover permanently?"

"Yes," answered Grame. "He will either recover permanently, or go to the other extreme permanently. Right now he is on the fence; very shortly he will fall one way or the other. He will be a perfectly normal human or as vicious a beast as you could imagine."

Grame paused a moment, then resumed: "He received a shock to-night in our fracas with the apes that will turn him in one of two directions. I firmly believe that we will know which direction it is before two days more."

"Good God!" I muttered.

There was something terrible about viewing a struggle between the human and the brute elements to win control of Nicky's small body.

"We'll have to watch him closely," I said.

"Yes, we will," replied Grame. "However, we must not hinder him from doing as he wishes. From what I know about his condition, he will attempt to return to the shattered group of apes at Large Island. If he does make the attempt, we must not prevent him; we must follow him. A battle will be fought in him between his human nature and his brute nature. And, mark me—we must not interfere in the battle in any way. If we do, all hope for Nicky is gone."

Grame's hands dropped and he sighed.

"Then we are not done with the band of apes?" I said.

"No," answered my friend; "we certainly are not."

CHAPTER XIX

A HURRICANE IMPENDS

MORNING FOUND THE island gloomy. A dark mass of clouds rolled overhead, and below the palm trees stood gaunt and lank, their fans drooping lifelessly like skeletons.

I had slept poorly. We had retired the night before after partaking of a slight meal the captain had had prepared for us. I was fortunate in having a very comfortable bed of boughs covered by a blanket. However, my rest had been disturbed by an oppressive sense of impending disaster.

Grame's statement about Nicky kept recurring in my mind, especially the fact that the child would return to the ape band at Large Island. We were free of the beasts now, and, with our increased numbers and supply of guns and ammunition, we could doubtlessly repulse any attack. But the fact remained that we were due to have further dealings with them, and under circumstances adverse to ourselves.

Breakfast served to cheer me up. Much to my surprise, our bill of fare contained both bacon and ripe bananas. The captain explained that he had run across the Mermaid, and had found her in very bad condition; at any moment the ship was likely to slip off the reef and sink in deep water. He and the men had taken many things from the boat. This accounted for the bacon.

The captain continued, in explanation of the bananas:

"You know, I believe some of the old pirates who used to have bases in these waters must have lived on this island. At any rate, there must have been a sort of plantation here. We have found all kinds of fruit trees growing wild. It will surprise you to know that we have oranges, bananas and scraggly pine-apple every meal. The bananas are good, the oranges a bit sour. However, they are very pleasant when eaten with salt. I recommend you to try the dish."

Breakfast over, I strolled aimlessly to the beach, where I sat down upon a drift log and watched the brooding ocean. The sky had become more overcast, and the surface of the water had assumed an ugly, oily aspect. As I looked at a small island to the west, I was struck with the fact that there was something queer about it.

In the first place, I could have sworn that it was not in the same position it had been last night. Besides, it differed in its entire character from all the other islands of this region. The vegetation on its shores was not composed of low, writhing mangroves, but towered up into the air, tall and straight, a solid wall of verdant green. Here and there were splotches of color, where some white or vividly red flower nestled among the leaves. Certainly vegetation of this nature was a strange thing in the West Indies.

I determined to take one of the boats and get a closer look at the islet. It was not far distant, and I had no doubt that the storm would hold off several hours.

As I started for one of the ape canoes, I saw Nicky in the distance, apparently unoccupied. Thinking it would be wise to give him something to think about, I hailed him, and asked him to accompany me. He assented readily and came skipping down to the beach.

"Where are you going?" he inquired casually.

"Over there," I said, pointing to the island.

"Oh!" answered the child. "I'd be glad to go with you."

As we approached the isle, I noticed that the deep water continued up to its very shores. This was odd; all of the other keys were surrounded by a narrow band of shallow water. As I was reflecting upon this matter and idly staring at the tall wall of green that frowned down upon the water at the island's edge, a sight caught my eye that made me gasp for breath.

There, swinging from a branch, was a snake twenty or thirty feet long, and a foot or more thick. Back and forth it swung, slowly and regularly. I sat spellbound, as powerless as a bird hypnotized by a reptile's beady glare. My glance could not penetrate the green wall that rose up from the very water's edge; but if it could have, what might not have been visible back in that dense jungle, whose advance guard was the frightful thing I had just seen?

In a moment or two I had recovered my composure. Raising a rifle to my shoulder, I took careful aim, and fired twice. The loathsome thing ceased swinging, slid downward, and vanished from sight. I had not missed my mark, but I doubt if the two bullets had any more effect than to wound the creature.

As I paddled along the shore, keeping at a safe distance, I caught sight of what I took to be a member of the leopard family—perhaps it was a panther. I fired a hasty shot at it, which was answered by a frightful scream.

My thoughts concerning the strange key were now taking definite form. The tropical jungle, the deep water surrounding, the python and the panther I had seen—all convinced me that this must be a floating island. It had probably drifted up from the tropics. It was not improbable that it had once formed a part of some mighty river's bank, and had been cut away by the current. Then it had floated down the river, and had been borne north by some ocean current.

I knew that such things did happen—the tangle of roots embedded in the soil would serve to keep the isle afloat, and it would withstand disintegration for a remarkably long period. Yes, this was undoubtedly a floating island. How else explain the fact that it had shifted position overnight? How else explain the presence of tropical foliage, and pythons and panthers? Such things do not live in the West Indian Islands.

And the apes? The mystery of their presence in this part of the world was explained. They had in all probability floated up on this island from the wilds of Central America, or even perhaps from the upper Amazon River.

As I was casting over in my mind the advisability of attempting a landing in such a place, I heard a sob behind me. Turning I saw Nicky with his head in his hands.

"Let's leave," he almost whispered. "The sight of that forest and those animals with their terrible cries—it makes me feel queer—like an ape."

I shuddered, and turned the bow of our boat toward home with all possible dispatch.

An odd thought occurred to me—here I was at the very roots of life. On one hand was the floating island, probably from the upper Amazon, alive with primal savagery. On the other hand was Nicky, at times as wild and fierce as anything upon the green-mantled isle. He had traveled backward through hundreds of centuries, and we had in him an antehominem being, a being wild, fierce and primeval. And both of these, Nicky and the island, had come thousands of miles to their bizarre meeting here in West Indies; and both bore with them their burden of elemental cruelty.

A pale yellow light had settled over islands and ocean, and in the distance were flashes of lightning, long and jagged. The dark clouds overhead were growing even more threatening, and the water all about suddenly became alive with phosphorescence. Here and there a dark triangular fin denoted the presence of a tiger of the deep.

A hurricane! I had never seen one, but if indications ever pointed clearly toward frightful storm, it was certain that these did. I seemed to be in a mood for odd thoughts. Could it be that some unknown power had brought these two symbols of savagery, the child and the floating island, together from the ends of the globe, and was now going to extinguish both with wind, waves, and lightning?

At all events, I thought, rallying out of my entanglement of fancies, we were in for a terrific hurricane and we would be lucky if we escaped alive.

CHAPTER XX

NICKY'S DECISION

AS WE MADE our way from the island, with the bow of the canoe bobbing to each stroke of the paddle, Nicky sat with his head in his hands. For several minutes I drove the boat ahead in silence reviling myself for having taken the child with me. The tropical verdure, with its pythons and panthers had affected him deeply. I wondered if he was going to lapse into his animal state then and there.

Then he spoke.

"It was I who threw you off the Mermaid," he said shortly.

I had suspected as much, but his outspoken confession astonished me. I merely nodded, and he continued:

"I pushed George overboard, too; I had been lying in bed right before I went on deck to do it, so when you felt under me the bed clothes were warm; and you thought I had been in bed asleep for some time."

The little devil had realized what I was about and tricked me thoroughly.

"You know," Nicky added, his face puckering quaintly, "I never know that I am going into a lapse until it is too late—I always want to tell father, or some one, that I am about to become terrible, but I just can't do it."

Nicky looked back at the brilliant green island a moment, then turned his face away. I spoke to him, but he did not answer; shortly afterward his little shoulders began to shake convulsively, and I knew that he was crying.

If a storm was threatening in nature, one was already raging in this child's mind.

We arrived at Captain's Island, with the storm still holding off. We were met by Grame and Dr. Meredith. I related to them what I had discovered about the floating island, and along whistle came from Grame.

"Of all the queer things we have encountered on this trip, this is one of the queerest. At any rate, it accounts for the presence of these apes. You remember I suggested that they might have drifted here on a floating island."

"Changing the subject," remarked Dr. Meredith, "it looks to me as if we might all be blown away. I think we are going to have a terrible hurricane."

We agreed with him, and set off for the camp to help arrange some sort of shelter against the approaching storm.

As we worked with blankets, limbs of trees, and stones found here and there, I kept a careful watch on Nicky. Knowing the effect the floating island had had on him, and remembering that Grame had said a crisis would come soon, I was afraid to let the child get out of sight.

And it was well I did have him under surveillance, for while the others were busied with some problem in constructing the storm shelter, I saw the child stalking through the woods toward the beach. There was no trace of stealth in his departure; he was leaving openly, and his firm strides bespoke a determination to reach his destination, whatever it was.

I called Grame to my side, and pointed out the retreating form.

"Humph!" muttered the doctor. "Let him go. Get Don, and we'll follow him. Arm yourselves with a rifle and three revolvers apiece. If we encounter any difficulties we don't want to be bothered with reloading."

"The apes again?" I asked.

"Probably," was his reply.

Grame spoke hurriedly with Dr. Meredith while I told Don to equip himself for action.

By this time Nicky was out of sight, so we set out over the ground that he had traversed. The course we followed was in the general direction of the boats. When we arrived we saw that he had taken one of the ape canoes, and was heading toward Large Island. We watched him several minutes. So intent he was upon his mission that he did not look back once. For that matter he turned his gaze neither to the right nor left.

"Come ahead," ordered Grame. "We'll take the Mermaid's dory and row after him. He is headed for the apes again. No doubt about that."

"Do you think he is going to join them?" inquired Don.

"Don't know," replied the doctor. "However, we'll soon see."

"I should think they would tear him to pieces on sight," I said. "Won't they remember he was largely the cause of their last disaster?"

"Maybe," answered Grame. "That is why we brought the arsenal with us. We've got to stick pretty close to him after he lands on the island."

"Think he'll see us?" asked Don.

"I believe he is so intent on getting to the apes that he won't notice us," I offered; and Grame agreed with me.

Nicky's canoe landed; he jumped out, dragged the boat onto the beach, and disappeared into the jungle. Redoubling our efforts, we rowed at top speed, and very shortly were landing ourselves. Taking time only to follow Nicky's example and beach our dory, we plunged into the jungle after the child.

He was not in sight, so we directed our pursuit from the noise of crashing twigs and swishing branches that came from ahead. The jungle here was comparatively open; almost like a forest. Nicky continued straight on in the direction of the pool. We passed one clearing which was littered with torn creepers and marked with many footprints.

"Here's where we had the battle last night," panted Grame.

The sight of the place filled me with thanksgiving that I was still alive. We continued on without a pause, and after a quarter of an hour or so, the pool came into sight.

By its edge stood Nicky, with his head in the air and a tense expression on his feature. He was evidently listening. However, he was not listening for us. We must have been creating quite a disturbance by our rapid travel, but he did not once turn his face in our direction.

He stood still for a minute, then set out up the lane between the trees.

"He's heading toward the cave," said Grame. "Let's stay in the woods, and go parallel to the lane. If we run we can get abreast of him, and be out of sight."

Following the doctor's suggestion we set out at a dog trot, and before long Nicky was directly to our right. Although his path lay clear and open, while ours was obstructed by vines and creepers, we managed to keep abreast of him. Before long we arrived at the face of the cliff that continued on to our old cave. Scaling its surface we continued our way along the ridge. Nicky was still on our right, and paralleling our advance.

Then we caught sight of the apes. Some two hundred yards ahead the cliff doubled back sharply, forming a large V. In the very apex of the V we saw huddled several of the beasts. How many had survived last night's massacre we knew not.

Evidently Nicky had not sighted the beasts yet, for he did not increase his pace. He was still forging ahead with that same plodding gait.

"Come on, boys," said Grame, "we'll get down on this side of the ridge"—pointing to the one opposite Nicky—"and run up to where the apes are lying. Then we can climb back to the summit and overlook the whole thing without being seen. Let's get there in a hurry so we can help Nicky if necessary."

We rushed along the slope of the ridge, plunging between closely placed trunks and tearing our way through labyrinths of creepers and roots. Our zeal was great, and consequently we managed to make very good time. When Grame judged that we had traversed about the right distance, he raised his hand to call a halt. Turning sharply to the right, we plowed back up the steep slope, and came out of the jungle behind a group of large rocks that seemed to be balanced on the very edge of the cliff.

Here was a perfect point of vantage. We could look to our heart's content without the slightest chance of being seen.

As I peered down into the cleft between the two opposing walls, an odd sight greeted my eyes. There, huddled up together at the foot of the cliff, were the remnants of the shattered monkey band. If dejection was ever written in the attitude of any group of animals, human or otherwise, here was one of the most striking examples of it I had ever witnessed.

With arms dangling lifelessly, and eyes gleaming dully, they squatted in utter silence. Not even a grunt or the motion of a limb disturbed the quiet. If it had been possible for me to feel pity for the brutes, I would certainly have experienced it then. They were crushed—their band had been almost demolished, and they seemed to be silently proclaiming their distress to the whispering forest near at hand.

Grame's voice cut into my thoughts.

"Eight," he whispered laconically.

The doctor was ever practical.

Nicky was not yet in sight. I found myself wondering what their reaction would be to his appearing. Then Grame spoke again, in an undertone.

"Better get ready with our rifles," he said. "We may have to do a little target work."

I thanked heaven that we were all good shots.

I squirmed about on my stomach till I was in a position to sight my Springfield on the band. Then I lay quietly with the muzzle of the gun resting upon a dead log in front of me, and waited.

A few moments passed, and Nicky came in view. He was

walking slowly, with his gaze glued on the little band below us. At first they did not see him; however, when he did attract their attention, pandemonium broke loose among the apes.

Up in the air they leaped and uttered weird, gargling noises. I interpreted these as expressing great joy. There they were, a ruined, crushed remnant, and their super-leader, by whom they supposed themselves deserted, had returned. Yes, it was joy that was being expressed by their fantastic antics.

Nicky continued his approach slowly. The apes, ceasing their leaping and howling, grouped together in a small knot and set up a hurried jabbering. Evidently they were deliberating what their course of action should be.

At length their chattering died away when Nicky stood only a few yards distant. One of the apes detached himself from the excited group, and loped toward the child. I say child, but the word is incorrect. At that moment he appeared a splendid, dominating brute.

The spokesman of the apes halted when he confronted Nicky, and with an uncouth flourish held forth a small baton. As Nicky hesitated, Grame whispered:

"My God, the royal wand!"

Nicky slowly accepted the baton, and regarded it speculatively. It was a remarkable picture. Under the fiercely lowering heavens in the midst of a dark green jungle stood the child-brute, while before him the huge ape leaned tensely forward, and the little knot of simians in the rear crouched together expectantly. And above them we three white men lay nervously behind our rifles; it seemed that every living thing in the place was waiting this one small boy's decision.

Don muttered an oath. Was Nicky going to accept the baton and return to his former comrades? The thought that the brother of my affianced bride was about to league with a band of wild animals almost stunned me.

The spokesman turned and made a sign to the waiting apes. Slowly they sank to their hands and knees, and then to their stomachs. I knew what was coming—the wriggling circle I had seen once before when Nicky had been crowned supreme chief of the ape band.

As I watched the boy's face closely I saw his expression, which had formerly been unreadable, change to bewilderment, and then to disgust. Very calmly he threw the little piece of wood to the ground and turned on his heel.

The big beast behind him uttered an ugly snarl, but Nicky began to walk resolutely away. The ape sprang after him. My finger crooked on the trigger, and in a moment more the monkey would have had a bullet through his head had not Grame restrained me.

"Don't shoot—yet," he ordered.

Nicky wheeled sharply; just in time. The ape stopped abruptly, held by Nicky's eye. I have never seen such a look as was on the child's face. Coolly and disdainfully he glared at his antagonist. The element of brute domination was there, but added to it now was the steely force of the human intelligence. The ape cowered back, and his comrades held their peace.

Nicky stood a moment piercing the apes with his ice-cold glance, and then walked away. He was not followed. A great throb of joy bounded through my heart when I saw him leave the apes of his own free will.

The human eye, plus a bit of sheer animalism, had held the brutes at bay.

"Well, I'll be hanged!" muttered Grame. "How did he do it?"

We retained our point of vantage for a few minutes to make sure that the apes would not recover from their apparent lethargy, and give pursuit to the child. However, they remained listlessly between the two cliffs and stared dully at the ground.

"Come on," said Grame at last. "Let's catch up with Nicky."

We made our way back by the same course we had come. Arriving at the opening of the lane we heard the sound of a person approaching. It was the child. I don't know whether he saw us or not, but he took absolutely no notice of us. Straight ahead he came, looking neither to right nor left.

"Shall we speak to him?" asked Don. "He doesn't seem to see us."

"Might as well try it," assented Grame.

As Nicky strode by I called his name. He turned and regarded us uncomprehendingly a moment, and then a happy smile overspread his face. He took one step toward us, held out his arms, and sank slowly to the ground.

Don and I rushed forward and lifted Nicky to his feet. He sank down again, unconscious.

"Where's some water?" asked Don. "We must do something to revive him."

"No," said Grame, "don't do anything to revive him. This is as it should be—Nicky has entirely recovered from, or rather permanently escaped, his affliction. When he awakens—for he is merely in a sound sleep—he will remember nothing of this, or anything that occurred while he was in the monkey stage."

He bent over the child and said:

"Well, let's take him home to Captain's Island."

But what I consider the strangest part of the whole business was not noticed by either Grame or Don. It was this—just as Nicky sank into the heavy sleep that told the story of his recovery—the sun broke through the clouds overhead, and the storm that had been threatening so violently never occurred.

CHAPTER XXI

ALL'S WELL

THE AFTERNOON WAS beautiful. The dark clouds of the morning had dissipated, and a cool sun shone down upon the glistening blue waters and green-mantled isles.

In the distance was the black smoke of a tramp which was steaming toward Captain's Island. It's attention had been attracted by a signal fire built by Dr. Meredith when he had first seen the smudge of smoke on the horizon.

As we stood by the pallet of blankets upon which Nicky lay, I saw his eyelids flutter.

"He's coming around," muttered Grame.

A moment more and the child's eyes were open wide. He stared at us vacantly, and then sat up.

"What's happened?" he muttered thickly.

"Don't bother about anything," said Grame, "you're all right, sonny."

"The wreck of the Mermaid!" Nicky exclaimed. "What happened? Where are we?"

"Don't try to remember," said Grame.

Turning to me he said: "That boy has been through the fire, but he is perfectly normal now." He stepped to Dr. Meredith's side, and the two conversed in low tones.

Eleanor, Don, and I left Nicky in his mother's arms, and walked down to the beach. As we stopped and watched the steamer's slow approach, I said to the engineer at my side:

"Don, you are scheduled to be a best man soon."

Don gasped in amazement, then smilingly extended his hand.

THE ARGOSY LIBRARY ™

SERIES 4 INCLUDES:

* TUTTLE * ENGLAND * FARLEY *

* BRAND * BRENT * ROSCOE *

* GIESY & SMITH *

* RUD * PETTEE *

* CUNNINGHAM *

THE BEST FICTION
FROM THE FRANK
A. MUNSEY LINE

Made in the USA
Middletown, DE
01 September 2020